M000031510

THE FREE
BRONTOSAURUS

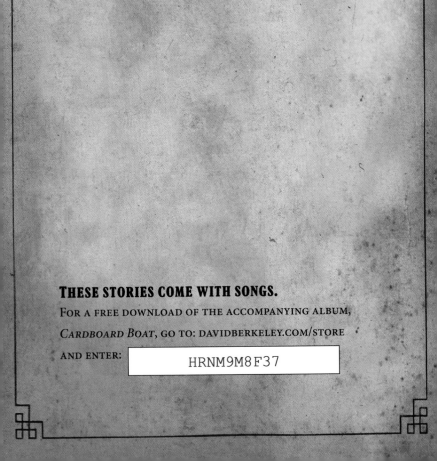

THESE STORIES COME WITH SONGS.

FOR A FREE DOWNLOAD OF THE ACCOMPANYING ALBUM,

CARDBOARD BOAT, GO TO: DAVIDBERKELEY.COM/STORE

AND ENTER: HRNM9M8F37

THE FREE BRONTOSAURUS

A NOVELLA TOLD THROUGH TEN STORIES, WITH TEN ACCOMPANYING SONGS

DAVID BERKELEY

THIS IS A GENUINE RARE BIRD BOOK

A Rare Bird Book | Rare Bird Books
453 South Spring Street, Suite 302
Los Angeles, CA 90013
rarebirdbooks.com

FIRST HARDCOVER EDITION

Set in Minion
Printed in the United States
Art and cover design by Luke Dorman

10 9 8 7 6 5 4 3 2 1

Publisher's Cataloging-in-Publication data

Berkeley, David.
The Free Brontosaurus : A Novella Told Through Ten Stories, with Ten Accompanying
Songs / by David Berkeley.
pages cm
ISBN 978-1-940207-98-8

1. Folk music—Fiction. 2. Folk musicians—Fiction. 3. Popular music—Writing and
publishing—Fiction. 4. Relationships—Fiction. 5. Family—Fiction. 6. Art—Fiction. 7. San
Francisco (Calif.)—Fiction. 8. Short stories, American. I. Title.

PS3602.E75645 .F74 2015
813.6—dc23

PART I.

THE FIND

"WHAT DO YOU KNOW about the legs of a brontosaurus?"

The security guard cracked a curious smile and then, as he typically did with Russell, ignored the question and handed him a lollipop.

"The legs," Russell repeated, unwrapping the Dum Dum. "They got any knees?"

The guard shook his head slightly and then threw up his hands. "Man, you are one crazy old fool. The hell do I know about a damn brontosaurus?"

Russell adjusted his thick frames and held the guard's gaze a minute, as if to challenge him to think harder about the question.

"Tell you what I do know. Bank don't open for thirty more minutes."

Russell was well aware of the credit union's hours. He was also well aware that a perfectly functioning ATM hummed idly only a few steps away. But Russell didn't trust computers. Nor did he believe in the hidden hand of direct deposit. "What you can't see you can't know," he liked to say.

"Aw, it doesn't matter anyway. Not anymore. Not with what I'm sitting on. Criminy, Jesse, wait until you get a load of what I stumbled upon a few days ago."

Russell bit off the lollipop ball in a single chomp, tucked the sweet into the fold between his back gum and cheek, and started sucking. He bent the stick into the wrapper and stuffed it into his pocket.

It was a method he'd honed during his years serving as Plainview's city archivist. Russell's supervisor didn't allow food or drink on the job. Was sure something would spill on or stick to an important document. That extended to lollipops, which Russell had clung to after quitting cigarettes.

Shortly after Lucy left, Russell took the position. Something to keep his mind off her. And for fifteen years, it more or less did keep his mind off her. Or at least it kept him busy. But then his eyesight began to go. Headaches came first. Then he started falling asleep at his desk. Soon he was cataloging paperwork all wrong, not catching typos. Blame the old green-screen computers and poor fluorescent lighting in his basement office. The city paid for his visits to the optometrist and his glasses, but he couldn't keep his job. Instead, Russell received a modest monthly disability check. The money allowed him to live. But there was nothing left to keep him sane.

Russell began spending hours and hours in the library. He started talking to himself. He drank multiple cups of coffee at the corner donut shop. He did crossword puzzles. He became an expert on local zoning laws and new construction projects. He went to all the public hearings on proposed developments, carrying a file folder stuffed with notes and evidence to support his positions, which were rarely that of the majority.

Russell and the security guard stood out there on the curb side by side a while. When it was clear the guard knew nothing about dinosaurs, Russell told him that if he ever wanted to borrow a VHS tape, all he had to do was ask.

"Now what the hell would I be doing with a VHS player, anymore?"

"Higher quality," Russell told him. "Quality over convenience."

The guard eyed him to see if he was serious and then patted Russell on the shoulder. "That's good, man. That's real good."

"You want to talk quality over convenience, Jesse, well then we should talk about the Mayans." And so the lecture began. Russell loved all lost civilizations, but he was particularly obsessed with the Mayans. He started in on the Mayan calendar and their system of astronomy. Then he appeared to drift away momentarily. This happened often when he went on about the ancients. He might space out for minutes on end. Sometimes he even cried. It also happened when something made him reflect on his life, on days gone by, on the people he loved, on those who abandoned him or those he drove away.

The guard didn't mind the silence. He started checking his phone.

When Russell snapped back into the present, he took off his glasses and wiped his eyes. He released a wheezy sigh, and said, "Man, I wish I were Mayan sometimes. Been all downhill since."

Finally, the credit union opened, and Russell barged in and passed the teller his check. Must have been a new employee, for Russell had never seen him before.

Looks to be all of twelve, Russell thought. *Is everyone younger than me now?*

"Just the deposit today, Mister...?

Russell cut him off. "Russell is fine. Rusty, if you prefer. Criminy, this isn't France," he said with an inappropriately loud laugh. Russell ducked his head and covered his open mouth with his forearm, something he did whenever he laughed or yawned. The move was meant to cover up his unusually large canines, which gave him a wolfish look when they appeared, frightening those who didn't know him.

The teller raised his eyebrows and leaned back on his stool. He took to processing the deposit. "Will that be all...Rusty?"

"Of course that's all. Unless *you* can tell me if a brontosaurus has knees."

The teller wasn't sure what to say. He turned to his manager. At least the manager was about Russell's age, something Russell appreciated. An honest man named George. Wasn't the most talkative fellow, but he'd processed Russell's checks on a number of occasions and could be trusted to make an accurate bill count. George nodded his head knowingly and motioned for the new kid to just try to finish the transaction. The teller counted the money quickly and passed Russell a slim envelope of twenties. Then he asked again if that would be all.

"Criminy, yes!" Russell said, far too loud. "That *will* be all. What else could I possibly want for now?" Russell looked over to George like he understood and then waived his hand dismissively at the teller, folded the envelope into his jacket pocket, and turned to leave.

He stiff-armed the door. "Ah, Christ, Jesse," he said as he walked out of the building. "Who even cares about the knees? Not with what I'm sitting on."

❖

ON THE DAY OF the discovery, Russell was up at 6:15 and out the door at 6:35. He was dressed as usual. Bomber jacket, faded gray suit pants cinched at the waist with a rope, tennis shoes, and a Russian fur cap that sat at a leeward tilt. The sun still had hours to go before it burned through the fog. He felt the moisture on his nose and lips, shivered slightly, pulled the fake-fur coat collar up, and hustled down the street.

Everything went as it always went for the first fifteen minutes or so. He noticed the same fading chalk drawings on the sidewalk, nodded his head to the same Chinese lady walking the same Shih Tzu, inhaled the aroma from the same patch of overgrown jasmine along the chain-link bordering the high school.

But as he rounded the corner at Virginia, something seemed different. Russell sensed it before he saw it. Soon bells were ringing wildly in his brain, and they only got louder and more reckless with every tentative step.

Russell rarely broke stride, but the farther down the block he got, the slower he walked. Eventually, when he reached the last house, he began walking in place. And then Russell stopped moving completely.

"What in the good God?" Russell whispered.

In front of a little, yellow stucco house, on an otherwise nondescript corner, beside a completely ordinary lamppost, among a few overgrown jade plants, stood a proud and wonderful stone brontosaurus.

"Criminy," Russell breathed, removing his hat out of respect. "Where did you come from?" He didn't wait for an answer. "And when?" he shouted. "I was here yesterday. I mean, of all the days, of all the gin joints!"

Russell approached cautiously, reverently, not quite believing it was real. He considered reaching out to touch the creature but thought better of it. He squatted down to look the dinosaur squarely in its painted eyes. Then he walked around it, fully around it, casing it. He took it all in: the capacious belly, the long, strong neck, the relatively tiny head.

"What a remarkable tail," he said at last.

Thinking about the physics of the huge wonder for a minute, he imagined the tail must provide a nice counterweight to that great neck. Balanced, sure, but what a troubling load to bear. He pictured lugging around a heavy length of garden hose.

What a burden, he thought, nodding his head with sympathy. Then he repeated it aloud, "What a real burden."

It must have been quite a relief, Russell decided, *to lie down at the end of a hard day and go to sleep, if in fact a brontosaurus slept lying down.*

Russell tried to recall what he knew about the sleeping habits of dinosaurs. Not a whole lot. Couldn't really imagine one of them splayed out beside a lagoon. Where would it rest its head? How would it stand back up?

Then Russell noticed those thick legs. Sturdy. Impressive. He thought first of the great columns holding up the Temple of Hephaestus. Then of the Giant Sequoias. "Well, come to think of it," he hesitated, "maybe it wouldn't be so bad to sleep standing up. The guy's like a big tree house."

Russell considered the new bridge being built. Probably would be a lot sturdier if they used this guy's legs to hold it up. He laughed hard at that thought, yanking his forearm up to cover his mouth.

"Well, that's strange," he blurted through the laughter. "No knees!"

It was true. The legs of the animal seemed to run straight down from belly to ground. He wondered if that was anatomically correct, searching his memory for images in old science textbooks, in magazines, in the city records, in cartoons, even. Images came, but they were fuzzy. And none was a photograph, of course, so he couldn't really be sure.

LATER THAT DAY, RUSSELL asked about it wherever he went. To the strange new librarian: "The legs of a brontosaurus, what do you know about them? Any knees?" She was writing in a notebook and didn't respond. He waited as long as he could, which wasn't all that long, and then threw up his arms and stormed out the door.

To the mailman sorting the mail into the boxes in his building: "You walk a lot. Like me. Think you could do it without knees?"

No response.

"Well, you ever wonder how the big dinosaurs did it?"

Still nothing.

Then Russell noticed the white headphone wires trailing from under the mailman's cap. Probably hadn't heard a damn word. Russell cursed technology and then half ran, half walked away.

To the waitress at the corner coffee shop: "Do they have knees?"

"Who?"

"*Who?*" He couldn't fathom how she didn't know.

"Yes, *who?*" she said. "Or is it *whom*? Do *whom* have knees?"

"Criminy, who has time for a grammar class? *The brontosauri* is who."

"The *brontosauri*?" she asked in confusion. "I have no idea, Russell. Jesus. Never thought about it. Sure, why not? They must have had knees."

Russell hustled back to the library, frustrated by his polling sample. Most of the dinosaur books were in the children's section. He pulled every one off the shelf and took the teetering stack back to his table. He removed his magnifying glass from his jacket pocket and flipped the pages furiously, mumbling about the evolution of the knee joint.

Reluctantly, he concluded that brontosauri did, in fact, have knees. Of course they had knees. But in many of the illustrations, it seemed the knees didn't operate like human knees. At least the front ones didn't. They kind of bent in reverse, more like elbows than knees, the forelegs bending forward not back from the knee joint.

He slapped the final book closed, put down the glass and looked up. "Well, okay. Fine. So they have knees! Big deal."

Russell also learned that there actually was no such thing as a brontosaurus. Apparently the "experts"—a term Russell always put in quotes—had recently decided to call the creature an *apatosaurus.*

"Well, not me," he vowed. "No, sir. Not me. Once a brontosaurus, always a brontosaurus." He added the new nomenclature to his lengthy and ever-growing list of the reasons he didn't trust science.

"First Pluto and now this," he said to the man sitting beside him. "What's it gonna be next, huh? They gonna tell us the Mayans didn't really invent hot chocolate? So they had knees," Russell continued, stacking the books on the metal return cart. "So he's not anatomically correct. So what?"

❖

WHEN RUSSELL HAD FIRST laid eyes on the dinosaur earlier that day, however, its lack of knees was just a minor curiosity, certainly not cause for alarm. Russell was so attracted to the odd creature, so mystified by his appearance, that details hardly mattered. Russell was in an altered state, feeling like an archeologist who had stumbled upon some lost city. In fact, he was so mesmerized, he didn't even notice the sign at first.

But after the shock of the discovery faded slightly, there it was. Clear as day. An index card rested against the dinosaur's front left leg with four large, black capital letters.

Russell read the letters individually.

"F-R-E-E."

Then he sounded the word out, like a child learning to read.

"F-r-e-e."

He bent down to get a closer look and read it again.

"Free."

Russell looked up from the card and removed his glasses. He looked up and down both sides of the block. He squinted up at the windows of that yellow house. Then he put his frames back on and looked down again at the card.

"Now what in the world could that mean?"

Free could be interpreted in any number of ways, of course, so Russell had to be cautious, had to think them all through. Understandably, Russell first read the sign as a proclamation of the wildness of the noble beast, his manifest destiny, his limitless domain. His was a time long before man, before fences, before sidewalks, before suburbs, before laws, before social pressures or judgment of any kind. His was a time before the Fall. No one was going to tell this god of the swamps how to behave. No, sir. He was free to do whatever the heck he damn well pleased. Free to roam and run anywhere. Free from responsibility. Free from all the shackles of society.

"You bet he's free!" Russell announced. "You betcha."

Russell put his hat back on and started to walk away. But the more he thought about it, the less comfortable he felt with his interpretation. Russell came to believe that it was an odd read. After all, the creature was made of stone and was only about two-feet tall by four-feet long, and that counted the tail. Then there was the knee situation to consider.

So Russell stopped and turned back around, trying hard to imagine how any other definition of "free" might apply. It stumped him. He had just about decided to give up when his eyes opened wide in wonder, in disbelief.

"Free?"

A few moments passed. Russell didn't move a muscle. Could it really be that simple? Would someone possibly just give this guy away? But why? It didn't make any sense. They didn't want anything in exchange? Not money? Not a different animal? Nothing? Russell mouthed the word *free* a few more times, getting increasingly excited.

He looked up and down the block once more. He tried again to see past the knickknacks on the window sill, to see if someone were watching, someone he could ask. He looked at the sky for a sign. He saw nothing. No one. He looked back down at the card.

Russell grinned broadly, shrugged his shoulders, bent at his knees, noting their importance as he did, and then, with a loud grunt, he hoisted the brontosaurus into his arms.

Well, he nearly threw the damn thing up and over his shoulder. The dinosaur was so light. Lighter by a long shot than Russell had estimated. What had looked so much to him like chiseled stone was just Styrofoam. It couldn't have weighed more than a pound or two. But no matter. He had it now, and he hugged the creature to his chest.

Russell felt something he hadn't felt in years. Twenty-two years to be exact, since he'd last seen Lucy, since he'd felt her skin against his. And when he put his arms around the belly of this Brontosaurus, he had to work hard to fight back tears.

"Criminy," he whispered, taking off his glasses and wiping his eyes with his fur cap. "I think he's mine." For the first time in a long, long while, Russell counted himself among the lucky ones.

He ran the three blocks home without stopping, except when he nearly collided into a woman pushing a stroller. Russell thought he recognized her from his building, but he had no time for pleasantries.

"Watch it!" she yelled.

"Not now!" he yelled back.

As the woman swerved, a tin box perched atop the stroller fell to the ground.

"Watch it with that tail," the woman said with a smile, swooping down to pick up the box. She brought it shyly to her lips and gave it a quick kiss. "Nearly got my son," she said, as he was stepping around her. "With the tail of that…what is that a…uh…brontosaurus?"

Russell mumbled something that sounded defensive.

"Well, alrighty then," she said and started to lean into her stroller. "Whatever it is, it's a little aggressive, no?"

"It's your son who's aggressive," Russell barked back as he sped off. "And a little big to be in a stroller, no?"

He realized he'd been rude. Out of her hearing range and still moving fast in the opposite direction, he hollered back over his shoulder, "Didn't mean that. It was our fault, of course, not your son's. Course it wasn't your son's. And yes, yes. A brontosaurus. A free brontosaurus. What are the chances?"

❖

RUSSELL MADE IT BACK to his building and climbed the stairs two at a time to the third floor without any more incidents. He didn't have a lawn of his own or he probably would have let the dinosaur graze. But that was okay. He knew just the spot for him. Tucking him carefully under his left arm, Russell removed his keys from his pocket and unlocked the door.

The place was a complete mess. Looked like he hadn't thrown anything away in over a decade. In fact, he hadn't thrown much away in over a decade. This dinosaur was definitely not the first thing Russell had brought home off the street. He crossed the room, maneuvering skillfully between half-finished model airplanes, binders of rare coins, stacks of word games and Sudoku books, and then slid open the glass door and stepped out onto the little balcony.

It was calm out there, the only calm part of his apartment in fact. The air was still damp, but the day was starting to warm up. The balcony overlooked the street and was flanked by two large oak trees. If he leaned dangerously over the railing and looked between the branches, he could see a slice of the water and a couple cranes near the new bridge.

In the corner stood three potted ferns that the former tenant had left behind. Russell half-expected someone might still come back for them, though he'd been in his place for nearly twelve years.

Scooting one of the ferns over a foot or two with the side of his leg, Russell placed the brontosaurus down lovingly and admired its outstretched neck, its mouth leaning toward some of those fingerlike leaves. He went into the kitchen to get a bowl. He chose one made of clay, which he thought seemed appropriate, filled it with water and set it down.

Russell stood there watching the sun trying hard to burn through the fog. He stayed with the dinosaur the rest of the morning, pointing out the various patches of blue as they appeared. "Lucy would have loved you," he whispered. "But that's okay. It's good. It's real good."

Eventually, he went off to the library to do his research.

❖

THAT EVENING, RUSSELL WENT back out to the terrace and sat down beside the dinosaur. This would become their nightly ritual. Russell looked forward to it all day. He began to feel like everything until then merely had been setting the stage for this brontosaurus to come into his life. Suddenly there was purpose.

"You know you can go whenever you like," Russell said, despite himself. "You know that right?" He waited for an answer. None came, so he continued. "Of course you know that," Russell laughed loudly. "I'm not gonna keep you down. I mean, who am I to keep a great guy like you down?"

The two of them sat there quietly late into the night. "Well, I guess it's time to turn in," Russell said, rising to his feet. "But in case it wasn't clear, I sure hope you'll stay. At least a little while. I really do."

FREEZER DRAWER

"TOTALLY REDONE," THE LANDLORD said as he led Suzie into the kitchen of the small, fourth-floor apartment. "Crown to corns."

Crown to corns, Suzie thought with a shudder. That was an expression she hoped never to hear again.

"And wait till you get a load of this brand spanking new fridge-freezer combo, sweetie!"

She didn't like the way the man said *spanking* or that he had called her *sweetie*. But that didn't seem reason enough to pass on the place. For the price, it was far better than anything else she'd seen, and Suzie had to admit the appliances did look shiny.

"I'll take it," she told him.

"Well now, hang on, sweetie," he said with a chuckle.

There it was again.

"How old are you?"

"I'm thirty-one."

His eyes traveled slowly down her body. "You don't look it."

Suzie didn't respond. She hoped to hell she wasn't blushing.

"Got a job?"

"I work at the Y."

"Credit?"

"It's good. It's great. Listen, I can get references. Please, I need the place."

"That's okay," he said, eventually, after looking her up and down again in a way that made her adjust her neckline. "Last name?"

"Gonzalez."

He looked at her another minute, like her name made some difference and laughed a strange laugh, which she didn't understand. "Rent by the fourth every month, or it's ten bucks extra a day. Late three months in a row and you're out, sweetie."

Suzie managed a thank you and told him that she and Charlie would move in that weekend.

On her way out, she saw a glimpse of herself in a mirror attached to the back of the bathroom door and paused. She rubbed at the bags under her eyes with her index fingers, trying to see her younger self in the reflection. Her hair was shorter than it had been, but it was still as dark. Like black coffee. When she was little it fell down to the middle of her back. Her mother used to call her Pocahontas, because of that hair and her eyes, which were just as dark, and because she used to run around the yard almost naked.

She turned profile, sucked in her breath and smoothed her sweater down over her stomach and thighs.

"What you looking at, sweetie?" the landlord hollered from the hallway. "You look great. Your reflection can wait. But I can't. Got to lock up now."

❖

FREEZER ON THE BOTTOM. Fridge on the top. "That's the way they design them nowadays," the creepy man had told her. "The newest thing," he'd said. Suzie took it for granted that the newest thing was the best thing.

But after two months in the place, she was done with that design. It made sense, sure. Heat rises. Put the coldest things on the bottom. She understood all that. Frozen foods get used less, so it shouldn't be such a big deal to bend down for them. It was sensible, but that didn't mean it was better.

"Stupid design," she'd say to herself every time she bent over for ice cubes.

The real problem, of course, was that the freezer didn't offer any real organizational system. It was more like a big freezer drawer, with a sliding half-shelf, like a frozen loft bed. Everything just lay there in one cold heap that shifted around each time she opened that damn drawer.

Often a bag of frozen peas or berries would catch as Suzie tried to push it closed. "Stupid design," she'd mutter. Then she'd have to yank the freezer drawer back out, shove the frozen mound around a little, and slam it shut again with her heel.

She mentioned it now and then to other residents she saw in the elevator or by the mailboxes. "It's a stupid design!"

But Suzie rarely got a sympathetic response, leaving her wondering why nobody else minded, whether she might be doing something wrong.

When Suzie was a kid, her freezer was on top—so high up she couldn't reach it until she was seven or eight. Her family also had an extra upright freezer in the basement. That freezer wasn't on the top or the bottom, it just was. Hundred percent freezer. *Crown to corns*, Suzie thought, with a grimace.

Everything was laid out so neatly then. Stocks and sauces in tall Tupperware containers on the top shelf. Breads and casseroles on the next shelf down in disposable tin loaf pans, wrapped tightly in foil and double bagged and closed with yellow twist ties.

She could still see her mother's script, written on the ripped strips of lined paper and taped onto the foil or the plastic lids. *Nobody writes in script anymore*, Suzie thought. *Dad's Three-Bean Chile 2/2/82. Bella's Chicken 4/8/81. Meat Lasagna 12/3/82.*

That freezer could have fed her family for months. Suzie's mother cut coupons, and so if there was a deal on buying in bulk, she bought in bulk. There was a shelf filled entirely with boxes of frozen peas. There were stacks of ravioli. Mrs. Paul's fish sticks and Swanson TV dinners. There were Pillsbury piecrusts. There was a whole Warhol of frozen Minute-Made Orange juice in the door. "For just in case," her mother used to say.

Periodically, her father would double up a couple Hefty bags and purge the most ancient items. Her mom never consented to this. She was of the old school, believing that once frozen, food would never go bad.

Suzie didn't actually want to eat any of that frozen inventory. She always had to put startling amounts of salt on the reheated soup for it to taste like anything. The freezer-burned meat was tough and dry. She wondered how anyone could like concentrated juice.

But no matter. Suzie wanted to stand before that towering open freezer door and feel the cold on her face again. She wanted to smell a meat sauce thawing on the stovetop. Wanted to hear the pop and hiss of that burgundy chunk as it melted.

She wanted to hear all the sounds in that familiar kitchen. Her sister going on about some boy, the news coming through the old AM radio that sat above the cookbook shelf, her mother humming a Carole King tune.

Suzie wanted to see her mother young again. Wanted to see that late afternoon light slanting through the lacy curtains, illuminating the yellow wallpaper with the bird pattern, the hanging orange pans, her mother's shoulders. That house had been sold years ago, and the freezer probably lay in some dump somewhere. Suzie imagined it standing out in the middle of a field littered with rusting auto parts under a hot sun. Suzie liked to believe that, despite the elements, it was still frozen and full.

Suzie was older than her mother was in those memories. Nothing in her life was there for "just in case." Every paycheck was cashed and spent. Everything Suzie bought at the store was cooked or, more likely, microwaved within days. It took all her energy to get to work, to make dinner, to tend to Charlie, to clean up the mess, to start again.

Charlie was her son. He was three, and he'd been an accident. On a second date with a man she didn't even really like. Suzie never admitted this to anyone.

But sometimes, when everything felt like it was closing in around her, when she was so tired the inside of her ribs ached, despite her best efforts, regret would creep into the corner of her mind, like a threatening stranger approaching on the sidewalk. Suzie would try to will the thought to the other side. Still, it found its way into her brain more often than she liked to admit, and it filled her with guilt for the rest of the day.

"I'm a good mother," she'd tell herself when the shadows fell. "Charlie's a good boy, and I'm a good mother…" She'd hug him extra long and hard after thinking those thoughts. It was impossible to hug him long and hard enough.

ONE AFTERNOON, CHARLIE WALKED into the kitchen hollering that he was starving.

"I'm *starving,* Momma. And the freezer's open, how come it's open?"

She didn't hear him.

"Momma, look." Charlie's dark curls were barely over the top of that freezer drawer. "It's still open, Momma!"

Suzie was staring absently out the window. "What's that, hon?"

"Momma, I'm *starving*!"

"Okay, okay. You don't have to yell."

"And the freezer's open! How come?"

She finally turned and spotted what he was talking about, cursed, and then shoved it closed. "Because it's a stupid design, that's why Charlie. It's a stupid, stupid design. And we hate it, don't we?" She gave it an extra kick, for good measure.

"Yes we do," Charlie said. "It's a stupid, stupid freezer." Then he used both hands and tugged it right back open to look for something he could eat.

"Close that, Charlie. There's nothing in there for you. I'll make you something. Hang on a sec."

THE NEXT EVENING, SUZIE went to the freezer to get a frozen pizza for their dinner. She pulled open the drawer. There was frost over everything. She cursed the damn design, pushed aside a bag of ice and a dented tub of ice cream and finally found the pizza on the very bottom. It stuck a little as she lifted it, making a "thwack" sound as she pulled it out. She flipped the box over and laid it on the counter.

"Oh my," she gasped.

Suzie smiled and let out a little giggle. No matter that the daycare attendant had told her Charlie had been misbehaving and asked if everything was okay at home. No matter that she could hear the neighbors yelling at each other through the walls. *Were those walls insulated at all?* No matter that she was still ten pounds heavier than she wanted to be and couldn't seem to lose the weight.

Suzie tilted her head and looked closer. Her smile broadened. She carried the box carefully into the living room where her son had plopped himself in front of the TV.

"Hey, Charlie!"

No response.

"Charlie. Hey, hey, come here. Come to momma. Look at this."

No response.

"Charlie, look! Look at this little beauty."

She had to hold the box directly in front of his chubby cheeks before he turned away from the TV.

"Honey, look. Look how beautiful it is!"

He didn't seem to know what he was looking at, so he looked into his mother's eyes, waiting for an explanation.

"It's a bird, silly. Don't you see it? It's a beautiful little bird."

"Where's the birdy?"

"See?" She pointed at the purple ice splotch. She showed him the wings, the head, the little beak. "You see it, don't you? You must see it."

"It's a birdy, Momma?"

"Yes, baby. It's a birdy."

"My shoe is off, my foot is cold," Charlie said.

"What was that?"

"My shoe is off, my foot is cold. I have a bird I like to hold."

"Where did you learn that?" Suzie asked with a smile.

"At school, Momma. Teacher Clara told me."

"Well I love it." She kissed him on the curls. "And if I can save this little guy, you can hold him."

She took it back to the kitchen, confused a little by how moved she was by this bird. Her stomach fluttered. She lay the box down carefully on the counter. Then she turned and pulled open the freezer to figure out where the little beauty had come from.

"It was the bag of berries, Charlie," she yelled over her shoulder. "Tipped over. The purple juice oozed out. That's what must have done it, honey. When the drawer didn't close last night, remember?" Charlie wasn't listening.

"Stupid design," she said to herself through a smile.

The frozen-juice bird seemed to have almost symmetrical wings, even a hint of a triangular beak. Some flaking pieces of ice suggested the contours of feathers.

She took the spatula from the drawer and began slipping it carefully between bird and box. She pressed down gingerly on the cardboard with the fingertips of her left hand, careful not to disturb the ice that was already beginning to melt around the edges.

As delicately as she could, Suzie worked the thin metal under the edge of the bird's wing. It rose momentarily. Suzie's heart pounded, hoping the bird might take flight. She slid the spatula in farther.

But then the lifted wing cracked. Maybe a centimeter above the bird's left scapula. It split off. Then the tail broke. And then, just like that, the whole thing was gone. Unrecognizable. Just a sticky, stained box remained with a few thin chunks of dark ice melting.

Suzie slammed her fist on the counter, hurting her hand. "I can't fucking do anything right."

Charlie came in and looked up with curiosity. Suzie was leaning back against the oven, her head in her hand. He asked what was wrong. She looked away, not wanting her son to see her crying. He asked again.

"Aw, it's nothing baby," she eventually said, wiping her eyes with her sleeve. She reached out absently to stroke his hair. She tried to regain her composure. "It's nothing. Momma just broke the little bird, that's all."

"What?"

"I said, 'I broke the bird.'"

"What bird?"

"The damn bird on the box!"

He flinched back and looked up, near tears. She bit her lip. "Oh, Charlie, I'm sorry. Come here, honey. You didn't…"

She kissed him and then scraped the remains into the sink. She turned the faucet on and watched the ice dissolve and disappear down the drain. She wiped the back of the box, smearing purple across the cardboard. She wiped the counter. She put the pizza into the microwave and pressed the door closed. She folded the box and stuffed it in the trash.

Noises began echoing in her head. The slam of the microwave door. The TV from the other room. The hum of the lights. Suzie stared out the window. The microwave dinged. An idling car revved its engine down on the street. She cut the pizza into bites, and her knife squeaked loudly against the counter. It gave her chills. She slid the plate across the table vacantly. Charlie didn't want to eat.

She threw up her hands. "Come on Charlie! Give me a break. You gotta eat."

She felt that old pit in her stomach, a little like an ulcer, except she didn't have an ulcer. She wanted to call someone, to hear a friendly voice on the line. But who? Her mother? How pathetic to cry to her mom about breaking some chunk of frozen juice on a pizza box.

"But it's not just the damn bird," she said to no one. "Who gives a damn?"

"You said *damn,* Momma. Teacher Clara says we don't say that word."

Suzie wasn't listening. She looked around her kitchen. It wasn't really the bird. It was everything. It was that stupid freezer drawer. It was the cold glow from those florescent bulbs. It was the stained carpet in the living room that her landlord refused replace. It was the crazy people living all around her. It was the weather. It was the mess everywhere.

"I don't want any more, Momma," Charlie said, pushing his plate away. He'd only eaten a few bites. "I'm done."

"Yeah, me too, baby. Me, too."

CHARLIE HAD ALREADY WATCHED more TV than Suzie normally allowed, but she let him watch some more. She half-heartedly tried to straighten up the mess. Then she brushed Charlie's teeth and helped him into a nighttime diaper and his pajamas. She lay beside him, her hair falling wildly around the pillow. She kissed his head. He tucked his little pudgy arm inside her arm and fell asleep. Utterly exhausted, she, too, began to drift off.

Just then, the bird returned. In that hazy half-sleep, Suzie saw it clearly, its wing healed, its tail intact, its feathers shining. The bird was bigger. Much bigger. It flew up off the box with a single flap of the wings, glided into the clouds and then swooped back down toward Earth. As it approached and came into focus, Suzie figured out why the bird on the box had meant so much.

"Of course," she mouthed. She knew what it was she had forgotten. She blinked her eyes open and propped herself up. "Jesus. How did I not see it immediately?"

She tiptoed quickly from Charlie's room, feeling suddenly wide awake. She rushed to her bedroom, dragged a chair to the closet, stepped onto it and reached up to the top shelf. She groped behind some sweaters until she felt it.

Suzie brought down a tin box. At some point it might have held a bottle of Scotch. There was a picture on the top of a harlequin playing an old stringed instrument. The box had belonged to her grandmother.

She clutched the box to her chest and carried it over to her bed. The lid was dented. The edges were rusty. It hadn't been touched in years. Propping herself up against the pillows, Suzie wiggled the top back and forth slowly and pulled up gently, as if worried something might escape. When the box finally popped open, she gasped.

There it all was: her old brushes, some charcoal pencils, a few erasers. Rolled tubes encrusted with paint.

She ran her fingers over and around them all. Then the tears came. They fell onto the rigid bristles and dry pastels.

"How could I have forgotten?"

Suzie was a painter. Used to be, at least. She painted portraits of people mostly. But she had an uncanny ability to paint animals, to capture their hidden strength, that mix of vulnerability and staggering power.

All the images came back then—the colors, the shapes, the feel of the thick paper. She shook her head. "My God, it's been so long."

When Suzie was young, she painted all the time. All through high school and some of college. But then what? Then there were parties, Suzie acknowledged. And there were boys. Well, and then Charlie came. And then she left that world, left a lot of things.

She sat up, holding the brushes. Her hands trembled slightly. She rubbed her fingers along the bristles, and then brushed the bristles against her cheek. She took up the pastels and then pressed the creased paint tubes into her palms. She brought them to her nose, inhaling the sharp, slightly metallic aroma.

Everything in the tin was unusable, of course, the brushes unyielding, the paints dried and brittle; still somehow her bedroom walls began to seem brighter.

Suzie knew what she had to do. First thing in the morning, after she dropped Charlie off at day care, she would go to the art supply store. She'd replace everything. Oh, if only the store were still open.

Lying back against the pillow, Suzie placed the still-open box beside her head. She closed her eyes, but she didn't fall asleep. She imagined prepping her canvas, mixing the colors. When sleep finally came Suzie dreamed she was back in her mother's kitchen, her little easel beside the stove and the fridge. She was painting a portrait of her mother wearing an apron covered with bluebirds. It was the best sleep she'd had in years.

PUZZLING

I T HAPPENED ONE MONDAY morning in late spring. The real beginning, however, could be traced back months earlier, to a lecture given by a visiting professor of botany from Peru. The talk was on shamanism, and Owen Hobbes was sitting in the front row.

Hobbes, as he was most commonly known, was a recently tenured physicist. Like many in his field, he was a tinkerer at heart. He liked to rebuild VW engines, ham radios, circuit boards, speakers. He was constantly running little experiments at home and in his office. There were computer parts strewn across his kitchen table. Petrie dishes beside the bed. He fermented cider. He tried to make cheese. He grafted fruit trees in his little backyard. It drove his wife mad.

"Owen!" Claire would yell upon finding something growing in a beaker in the bathroom. "You have a lab, you know!"

Hobbes enjoyed training his eye to deconstruct his field of vision. Big to small. Buildings within the city. Blades of grass within the field. Then smaller still. He'd imagine the cells, the molecules, the atoms. He would reduce all he saw into parts and pieces, like a Pointillist painting, and then like another Pointillist painting within every given point. Eventually, he'd rest in the space between, "the vast space between," as he liked to call it.

"Don't be fooled," he'd tell his students. "That space between is not nothing. It's absolutely everything."

His work focused on proton decay. He and his colleague Carl were trying to counter the common belief that protons were stable and couldn't be divided into smaller parts. This never sat well with Hobbes, a man who believed everything that existed, everything that had matter, could and would break down. "That's part of what's required to be matter," he explained, "that it be divisible and impermanent." He'd add with a twinkle, "That's all that matters."

The research wasn't going very well, though. And maybe it was frustration that led him out of the lab and into the lecture hall that evening. In a thick accent, the Peruvian scientist explained his theory that South American shamans learned their medicinal secrets through drug-induced visions. He argued that deductive reasoning never could have yielded their troves of knowledge. "Not in ten thousand years of rigorous and organized work," he said. That number resonated with Hobbes. "Hallucinogens," the lecturer asserted, "were the key. And they still are the key." He held that a set of naturally occurring psychedelics helped shamans actually communicate with plants, access a universal knowledge, interpret the language of the Earth itself.

Although not exactly an uncommon hypothesis, it was poorly received in a university lecture hall full of Western scientists. Most thought the professor a quack.

Many walked out. Hobbes, however, sat rapt. He had read articles on the subject, but none had affected him like this lecture. Even right there in the big hall, he began picturing a plant's energy field. He envisioned the floor cracking open and the seated scientists falling in as a large banyan tree grew up and filled the room, as vines spread and twisted around the spotlights.

Hobbes waited while the remaining faculty streamed out of the auditorium. He approached the scientist, thanked him, and offered to walk him back to where he was staying. Hobbes took him for a drink, which led to a stroll around town, which led to an all-night conversation on a park bench. When Hobbes turned the lock in his front door and crept toward the bedroom, the sky was already lightening.

Hobbes scribbled down all the titles on shamanism the scientist had referred to, and over the next two weeks Hobbes read them all. He became increasingly fixated on the ayahuasca root. When prepared properly, the professor had told him, it was among the strongest substances the shamans took.

For a while, Hobbes tried to convince his wife to take some with him. They'd done LSD together when they were dating. Claire had wanted to go to the ocean and swim, to feel the sand beneath her feet, to just lie on a blanket looking at clouds. Hobbes had wanted to be more scientific about it, to stay inside taking notes, documenting his every mood and thought. He wanted to chronicle his visions, to understand the chemistry happening inside his brain. Apparently, that turned Claire off to doing serious drugs with Hobbes again.

So he moved on to Carl. His research partner was a junior faculty member of the department. Hobbes had gotten him the job. They met when Carl was just a bewildered grad student and Hobbes was finishing his postdoc. They became fast friends. Claire had even introduced Carl to the woman he eventually married.

Hobbes didn't really expect Claire to try Ayahuasca with him, but he was pretty sure Carl would. Their work had hit such a wall, he figured Carl needed the release as much as he did. The subject came up almost every morning for a couple weeks.

"Something to take our mind off those blasted pions, Carl. Come on! When was the last time you loosened that tie?"

But Carl resisted, and so eventually Hobbes stopped pressuring him. Decided to just take it alone. So on an otherwise-ordinary Monday, Claire away at a sales convention in Atlanta, Hobbes awoke early. He had no classes to teach until the next afternoon. He washed his face, looked into the mirror a little longer than usual, and then brewed a pot of hot water. He would make the Ayahuasca tea from a powder he'd been preparing in his lab. As was recommended, he had fasted the previous day. Intending to take notes on the experience, Hobbes had a new composition book open to the first page. The teapot whistled, and he could hardly contain his nervous excitement.

THE NEXT MORNING, CARL showed up at the house as he always did when they both had early classes to teach. Rounding the corner onto Hobbes' street, he expected to see him waiting impatiently out in front of his clapboard house, ready to spout some new theory about bosons. He grew suspicious, though, when he made it all the way to the front door. Carl pushed his horn rims back up the bridge of his nose and hollered. He rapped on the door.

"Fuckin' Hobbes," he said to himself as he turned his back to the house and waited. "I have a ten o'clock. You do, too."

He banged again, zipped and unzipped his jacket, paced on the porch.

"You coming or not? Jesus, man, what are you doing in there? You dead?"

But when Carl peered through the window, he gasped.

Books and a shattered lamp littered the floor. A side table was overturned. Carl pressed his face harder against the glass, trying to see more.

New panic in his voice, he tried again. "Hobbes? The hell is going on?"

Finally, he spotted his friend slumped over in a chair. Carl cursed under his breath, hoping, half-heartedly, that it was some sort of sick prank. He yelled out.

No answer. Hobbes was dead. His mentor. His best friend. Carl felt the air go out of his lungs. His knees buckled. He heard an airplane overhead; someone bounced a basketball on the sidewalk down the block. Then a police siren whaled somewhere in the distance, and Carl blinked back into focus. He shook his head and tried the door. It was unlocked. He rushed in, checked for breathing.

"Oh, Jesus. Thank God," he cried. "Shit, Hobbes. What the hell happened?"

But there was no response. Carl shook him. He pleaded with him to wake up. He slapped his face. He had no idea what to do. He ran to the sink for a cup of water and threw it at him.

Finally Hobbes jerked his arms, coughed, blinked a few times, and flinched awake. He squinted. He gasped. He coughed some more. He held his stomach and groaned.

"What the...?" He thrashed his arms around and shook Carl's hands off him. "What are you...?"

"Hey, hey. Easy. It's Carl. It's Carl here."

Hobbes didn't respond.

"It's okay. You're okay."

"Who the...?"

"Just relax, Hobbes. You'll be okay."

Hobbes' eyes were wild still, unable to focus. He scanned the room. He was chewing on his lip. He began saying something, but Carl couldn't make sense of it. Everything was wrong. He called 911. He called Claire.

Waiting for the ambulance to arrive, Carl remembered this upright piano being moved into a building he once lived in. The movers dropped the thing down an entire flight of concrete stairs. The noise was tremendous. Carl had seen the thing busted apart at the bottom of the stairwell, its lid broken off, the soundboard cracked in two, most of the strings snapped.

Claire took the first flight she could book back from Atlanta. She discovered a notebook, but it was mostly illegible, full of strange drawings and odd symbols. The first few entries were clear.

10:20 a.m.—Consumed 400 ml of tea. Rancid taste of dirt or tree bark.

10:28—Upset stomach. Slight nausea. Dull pain on right side below rib cage.

10:51—Nausea becoming severe. Seeking fresh air. Opened window. Washed face. Perspiring heavily. Teeth chattering. Tingling hands. Textures and patterns more pronounced. Lines of separation blurring.

11:03: Swinging pendulum. Time slowing. Color. Intense color. Left side of jaw numb. Visions intensifying. Circularity of time.

11:13: Swing set. Dad. Flying. Serpent eating tail.

11:22: Very cold. Can't feel face.

His handwriting worsened with each entry. Soon it was just scribbles and pictures, patterns, illegible notes.

OWEN'S HALLUCINATIONS HAD STARTED small and manageable, but eventually everything began to unravel. Sounds got louder. Thoughts began to warp and echo. The pendulum of the grandfather clock across the room appeared to slow down and then speed up. His mind, like the clock, would race, as if all the thoughts that he had ever had flooded back, uncontrolled. Then the chaos would stop, and he would fixate on a single image or thought with piercing intensity. He held it, rotated it around, examined it from every imaginable angle.

An image came of a tree swing. Owen could hear a child's voice, which he soon recognized as his own. He was on that swing, and his father was there pushing him. Everything had a sepia hue. There was a radio playing oldies through an open window. But then his father was gone, and Owen began swinging faster, higher, too high. He didn't know how to get off. He was scared and screamed for his dad.

Soon the nausea grew intense. He wanted to vomit but couldn't will it to come. He grew dizzy, aware, it seemed, of the Earth's spin.

Then Owen was suspended in the air. He'd had flying dreams before, but nothing even close to this. He felt the wind in his face. His eyesight became incredible. In a bright glimpse, he could see it all, different perspectives at the same time, the other side of the world even. He saw the roof of his childhood home. He saw Plainview's skyline. He saw the outline of North America.

And there was the Pacific. Oh, the Pacific. He had never seen anything so beautiful. He began to cry. Euphoric tears. The color was richer than he'd ever imagined. Blue first. Then indigo. Pure indigo. It pulsed and radiated. It had depth and contour, almost like velvet. He wanted to enter it, to merge with it.

But then everything became still. The indigo darkened to black, and Owen became very aware of how small he was in relation to that great sea below him. He felt utterly alone. The air thickened, and it became hard to breath. It felt like his heart had stopped beating. Perhaps it did for a time.

Owen began to fall, blisteringly fast. Through the sky. Through the water. Through the ground beneath the water. Through the center of the Earth. Then out the other side.

His stomach was working to get out his throat. He flapped his arms up and down, trying to fly, to stop falling. His arms hit things, bruising and cutting his limbs, breaking the lamp. But the flapping didn't stop his fall. He grasped for something, anything.

Owen's heart pounded. He worried his heart would actually explode. The beating grew unbearably loud. He didn't know if it was the clock or his heart. His body poured sweat. He was dying of thirst. His head felt like it might split apart. He could hear his own voice. Thoughts were coming so fast. Too fast. He fell back into his chair. He blacked out.

❖

THE NEXT FEW MONTHS passed in a fog. Carl tracked down the guys in the chemistry department who had procured the drug. That helped piece together at least part of the story. They were able to test the root. It wasn't tainted, but it was unusually strong. In fact, they said they'd never seen a strain so pure and strong. Considering that Owen had distilled it further and had been fasting, the severity of his reaction made more sense. Still, everyone was surprised by how long the effects continued.

Owen certainly couldn't drive, couldn't be trusted alone at all. So Claire took him to one specialist after another. They put him on a parade of drugs. Risperidone. Lithium. Clozapine. Nothing worked. If anything, they made him worse. One made him highly emotional and irritable. Another numbed his emotions. One gave him heart palpitations and made his hands shake. Another took away his appetite. Owen lost fifteen pounds that first month.

He couldn't sleep. He felt always on the verge of a discovery. But the discoveries never came. He went for walks. He'd try to tell Claire what it was he saw, but the images were mostly isolated, incoherent. It was hard for her to tell truth from fiction: rabbits all over a car, a bridge to nowhere, a swinging pendulum. He mentioned the pendulum all the time. Claire didn't understand what he was seeing, what he was trying to say.

Owen Hobbes had lost his mind. His thoughts stayed jumbled. Unable to articulate what he saw and felt, he stopped trying.

Claire was patient at first, even loving. She encouraged him to talk, to try. And she tried to listen. But after a while she grew irritable. She would bolt awake, unsure what was wrong. Owen would be sitting up in bed. She'd see those once-sharp eyes staring vacantly into the blackness or, worse, staring at her, and it was terrifying.

"Ah, Owen! Jesus. What are you looking at? Please. Please, just go to sleep."

It was pretty clear by late July that, barring something miraculous, Hobbes would not be teaching in the fall. He took a temporary leave from the college. That turned into a permanent leave. Claire suggested that he not go downtown anymore. Then she suggested that he not leave the house anymore. And then she left him.

One morning in October, Owen unshaven and in a bathrobe, the sky heavy, like it might finally rain, Claire found the courage to say it.

"I'm leaving you, Owen."

Somewhere inside him there was shock. But he said nothing.

"Can you hear me, Owen? I said, 'I'm leaving you.'" She grabbed him by the arms.

He tried to speak. But what was there to say?

"Say something! Please, just say something."

She was crying. He still couldn't find the words.

"I can't do this anymore! God, Owen, I can't even tell if you hear me!"

Still nothing. She waited as long as she could. The silence was awful.

"I just…I'm sorry, Owen."

So she left. A bag in each hand, she walked out the door, across the porch, and down the steps. Owen followed her to the edge of the porch. Turning back before getting in the car, she thought she saw tears forming in the corners of his eyes. It looked like he was trying to say something. She stood there terrified but half-hopeful.

He took a big breath, like a diver about to spring from the board. His chest rose. Claire waited. She took a tentative step back toward him. But then his chest caved back in. His shoulders slumped. Whatever had sparked in Owen, whatever it was that had tried to fight its way up through the layers, retreated again. Owen's head drooped, like a sunflower in late autumn. The moment passed.

That instant broke her heart. It almost made her drop her bag and go running back to him. It took everything she had to make it to the car, to turn the key, to hold onto the wheel, to keep her eyes on the road and not the rearview. Owen went down the steps, but he got no further. He watched the car pull out and then recede, until it disappeared around the corner.

Owen stood there like that in their small front yard most of that day. Neighbors saw him. He was a big man; well over six feet tall and wearing only his bathrobe, he was a disturbing sight. A dog walker asked if he was okay. A father passing by with his kids ushered them to the other side of the road. The lady across the street almost called the police. Owen just stood there, staring in the direction Claire had driven, unresponsive under the iron-colored sky.

❖

THAT WINTER WAS HARD. Really hard. Owen almost died. He probably would have if Carl hadn't come to check on him every Sunday. Carl made sure that Owen had his medicine and food in the refrigerator.

They had a routine. Carl would bang on the door. Then he would call out: "You dead, Hobbes?" He'd turn the key. "It's Carl here."

Carl brought groceries. He'd cook him something that would keep for a week. He'd take out the trash. He'd remind Hobbes to change clothes, to take a shower. He'd update him on the research, though there was little to report. He tried to make conversation, but mostly Carl just talked to himself.

"Hard to believe how much actually goes into holding it all together," he might say. "Hard to believe how fast it all can change, you know? It's like some scaffolding, some unseen skeleton, keeps it all upright." Hobbes wouldn't respond. Might not even be looking at Carl. "Like thousands of involuntary muscles work to keep the tension, to keep a world intact. And in an instant, in just about any instant, it can all snap, uncoil, unravel, go slack."

Eventually, Owen developed a routine, doing the bare minimum required to survive. Shaving was not in that category. His stubble went gray and soon became a beard. It grew and grew, like blackberry brambles, eventually consuming the lower half of his face. Neighbors started calling him Boo Radley. They had their theories about what had happened to him, about the dark secrets he was hiding, about how much he must drink, about what crime he might have committed, about what he had seen in Iraq or Bosnia.

Owen might emerge suddenly out of his front door and rush up the street. Other days, he'd just walk out slowly and wander aimlessly. Maybe he'd bend over and stare at a crack in the sidewalk for a while. Or he'd sit on a bench at a bus stop but wouldn't board the bus when it came. Maybe he'd look at a morning glory with great wonder. Or he'd weep at a dead bird in the road. Sometimes he was full of joy, almost bursting with it. Other times his lips would quiver as if he wanted to say something or had seen a ghost.

There were days of relative clarity. But on those days, he felt a terrible loneliness. He longed for the energy he used to have. "For Christ's sake," he'd say to himself. "I'm only forty-six years old."

Since the breakdown, he looked at least a decade older. His former life would pass across his mind, like the shadows of clouds he'd seen once driving through the desert. He'd remember part of a joke he used to tell. He'd recall an argument relating to his work. He'd hear the sound of his own laugh in some recess of his brain. Sometimes, at night, he'd call out for Claire, confused about why she wasn't beside him in bed.

❧

THEN, ONE SUNDAY IN March, the hemlock just starting to bloom, Carl showed up with a jigsaw puzzle in a shopping bag. The idea had come from a note scribbled on doctor's stationery he'd found while straightening up the kitchen. It read *FOR ANXIETY* and listed a few suggestions.

"Something good for the nerves," the head doc had told Claire in the hospital "Maybe painting or needlepoint?"

Needlepoint had been a curious suggestion, and even under those circumstances, Claire had smiled.

"Or puzzles," one of the nurses added. "Puzzles are very soothing, Mrs. Hobbes."

So that's what was listed there on the note: *Needlepoint, painting, puzzles.*

Carl couldn't help laughing picturing his friend embroidering *Home Sweet Home* onto a pillow. But puzzles. Well, now that was another matter. "Of course," he mouthed. Carl imagined that Hobbes could have done puzzles blindfolded.

The very next day, Carl bought a jigsaw puzzle at the one store in Plainview that still sold actual board games and then just left the box on the kitchen counter.

Owen found it a couple days later with a note on it.

> *To Hobbes,*
> *For when the time is right*
> *and you're ready to put*
> *the pieces back together.*
> *Carl*

Owen held the box in his hands for a long time. The image was of a few dozen hot air balloons in a bright blue sky. Eventually, he slit the shrink-wrap and opened the top. The pieces were in a plastic bag. He ripped that open as well and breathed in the air. Owen thought he detected the scent of the high desert, of piñon and sage.

Puzzling was what he came to call it, and it quickly became all Owen did. It proved to be more than soothing. That first puzzle and those that followed were cathartic, transformative, magical.

His method was always the same. First, he looked long and hard at the image on the box, memorizing the picture, the shapes, the colors. Then he opened the box, closed his eyes, and inhaled deeply. He scattered the pieces, his hands hovering for a few moments after turning them all right-side up, like a hawk scanning a field for mice. His fingers twitched, as if they themselves could see. He studied the pieces, rearranged them in his mind, envisioned how they fit together.

Then Owen would begin. And once he began, he hardly ever paused, somehow knowing where the next piece went before he placed the one in his hand. He rarely worked from the edges, finding instead patterns and patches in the middle. He built out from these little islands, eventually connecting them all. He was methodical, deliberate, consistent, steady.

Graceful. That is really what he was. There was grace in how his hands floated above the pieces, in how nimble his fingers were. Though vacant for so long, his watery blue eyes locked into focus again when he was at a puzzle.

The most remarkable part of Owen's methodology, though, was what he did as soon as he had finished. Just as the scene was whole beneath him, he immediately began to disassemble it. As if completion had never been his goal, as if there was no need to celebrate his success, as if he knew the image so well that he didn't need to admire it.

Nothing in the dismantling was aggressive, reckless, or impatient. Owen was gentle about it, just as deliberate taking it apart as he had been putting it together. He tried to make each scene disappear as smoothly as it had appeared, inch-by-inch, piece-by-piece. Indeed, he wanted to remove the pieces in the exact opposite order that he had placed them. Some kind of reverse evolution. This process never worked perfectly, but it was always his goal.

Soon Owen was buying jigsaw puzzle after jigsaw puzzle, great puzzles, with as many pieces as possible. *Six thousand. Ten thousand.* He became a regular at the little gaming store downtown, if the strange set of men who frequented that store could be called *regulars. Star Trek* fanatics. Old men still obsessed with *Dungeons & Dragons.* Teens who wore long black cloaks and played collectible card games. Even in this crowd, though, Owen stood out.

His eyes brightened whenever he entered the place. The two boys behind the counter, of course, noticed him. Like Owen's neighbors, the clerks had their theories about him. One thought brain trauma. The other, a psych student, believed Owen suffered from a depersonalization disorder. Whatever the diagnosis, they tried to be kind.

One day he awkwardly approached the register, laid his large hands on the counter and, in a hoarse voice, said, "I'd like you to order me the biggest puzzle you can find."

It was the first time either of them had heard him speak. They were surprised by the dryness of his voice. And though they imitated that sound and his mannerisms long after he left, they were both secretly happy that he had spoken to them.

One of the clerks called Owen a week or so later. The phone scared the hell out of him.

"Yes?"

"Uh, Mr. Owen?"

"Hobbes."

"Hobbes?"

"Hobbes."

"Oh right, right. Sorry, Mr. Hobbes." The boy was nervous. "Was reversed here on the order form." He tried to make pleasantries, asked him how he was doing and then regretted the question.

"Who's this?" Owen asked slowly.

When the clerk told him, Owen loosened his grip on the receiver.

"Well, uh, we got a puzzle in that we think you might want to have a look at."

Owen hung up the phone and put on his socks and shoes. He made it to the shop in about half the time it usually took him.

The puzzle was of the pyramids in Giza. It had 33,000 pieces. The box was made of wood. The whole thing weighed almost thirty pounds. Hobbes had to move the furniture around in the living room so he could do the puzzle on the floor.

It was by far the hardest puzzle he'd ever attempted because the sand and the bricks all blended together. Every piece looked virtually identical. It took him ten days to finish. Then Owen went back to the store. He didn't say anything at first, but something was different in the way he held his head and shoulders. The boys behind the counter noticed, thought he looked taller.

"Did you like it Mr. Hobbes?"

"Could you do it?" the other asked

"Could I?"

"You liked it then?"

"Did I?"

They looked at each other nervously. One raised his eyebrows at the other.

"But it was…well, it was all sand," he went on when he gained his composure. "The thing was all sand."

They nodded, unsure whether this was good or bad.

Owen told them that it was the greatest puzzle he'd ever seen, maybe the greatest ever made. They detected joy in his voice for the first time.

"We're really glad you liked it," one said.

"Pretty sure no one else but you could ever have done it, Mr. Hobbes."

Hobbes' lips slowly formed a smile. The smile turned into a laugh that went on too long. He began to cough and grasped the counter until it passed. When he finally looked up at them, he had tears in his eyes. "Thank you, boys. Thank you."

SLOWLY BUT STEADILY, ONE puzzle at a time, summer gave way to autumn, and Owen became increasingly coherent. He started talking more and more with Carl, started conversing with people on the street, in the library, at stores.

On the first Sunday in November, when Carl approached the house, Owen was on the porch deadheading a geranium. Some Halloween decorations still brightened the neighborhood. It was the first time in twelve months that Owen had been outside when Carl arrived.

"You dead, Hobbes?"

"Not yet, Carl. Not yet."

"It's been a year, Hobbes. Believe that?"

Hobbes just shook his head. "Feels like I still have this hole in my heart, though, Carl."

Carl nodded. He got up to get a couple glasses of water. He didn't know what to say. "I can only imagine." Carl watched a guy in a Russian fur cap walk by talking to himself. "But it's filling back in, Hobbes. Little by little, no?"

Eventually, they spoke about the weather, the lack of rain. Carl started talking about the new bridge. "Be open soon," he told him. Small talk. They'd been doing that for a few weeks. It was awkward, but getting easier.

There was a long silence. Carl finished his glass of water. Then, looking at his feet, he said, "I think Martha and I are through."

Hobbes looked confused. "Martha?"

"My wife."

"I know, Carl. But what are you talking about?"

"It's been bad for a while. I haven't said anything."

"Why?"

"Why? Because you were…well, because I just didn't…"

"No. Why's it bad? What's the matter?" Owen's responses were slow but appropriate.

"I…I'm not sure, Hobbes. I'm not sure."

They spoke about it for a few minutes, as much as Owen could manage. Carl didn't exactly get what he needed, but it still felt good to let his old friend know what had been going on at home.

Owen wasn't exactly in a place to offer advice. Carl knew this. After a while, he asked Carl if he wanted to do a puzzle.

"Supposed to be a good one. Dinosaurs."

Carl hesitated but then said, "Sure. Why not? Loved them as a kid."

"Puzzles?"

"Well that, too. But, no, I used to be crazy about dinosaurs."

As he said it, Carl thought again of Martha. He shook his head. "I think I blew it, Hobbes. I think it was my fault."

Carl stayed another fifteen minutes or so. He watched as Hobbes arranged the pieces, like a tai chi master or a conductor of a great orchestra. Carl stayed out of the way, more or less just kept Hobbes company, marveling at his method.

When Carl finally got up to leave, he felt lighter. More hopeful. Owen walked him to the door. And then without warning, he pulled Carl in for a hug. "Thank you, Carl. You saved me. You know that right?" His voice cracked with emotion. And then as Carl was closing the door, Owen added: "Maybe you can still save things with Martha."

That made Carl break down, something Owen had never seen. Carl turned back to his friend, took off his glasses, managed a smile, and then shrugged his shoulders.

"Thanks Hobbes," he said as he turned again to go. "I've missed you." Owen watched him walk away. Then he closed the door and went back to the table to finish the puzzle.

THE NEXT DAY WAS the day of the earthquake. Owen sensed the danger seconds before the shaking began. He felt it first as a curious wind coming through the open kitchen window. He heard dogs all around the neighborhood barking and howling. Then the shaking began.

The loose puzzle pieces began bouncing up and off the table. Owen crawled under that table, and the pieces fell down around him. The whole prehistoric scene slid off and broke apart. It seemed the house itself began to sway. Every dish, glass, book, and picture started to rattle.

One window in the bedroom shattered, some of his grandmother's china crashed from a kitchen shelf. The bookcases fell over. A wedding picture still on display cracked. Test tubes and beakers broke as well. But incredibly, when the walls stopped moving, they were still intact. The roof held. The house was okay. Owen eventually was able to stand. Dizzy, he stumbled onto the street.

There was dust in the air. Trees and power lines were down. A tall palm tree that had no place even being there in the first place had been uprooted. Took out three cars. Everything was eerily quiet, strangely peaceful. With the power out, the lines weren't humming. There were no radios or televisions on. But then sirens came from several directions. People screamed.

Owen ran his fingers through his beard, startled by how long it had grown. He looked at his reflection in a car window and almost didn't recognize himself. Staring back up at his house from the cracked-up sidewalk, he saw that a gutter had detached and a downspout had fallen, some bricks from the chimney knocked loose. *Could have been a hell of a lot worse*, Owen thought.

An aftershock came a few minutes later, nearly knocking him from his feet. Owen steadied himself on the railing until it was over. He took a deep breath, grateful that he was still standing. Then he headed back into his house to begin picking up the pieces.

FOUND ART

SHEILA DID NOT HAVE a temper. She didn't hold grudges. She never sought revenge. She was a pacifist, after all. She was opposed to every war, even the second world war. And there weren't a lot of people who admitted to being against that war. She bought local. She did yoga. She lugged around her own water bottle and tea mug. She drove an art car, for Christ's sake.

But maybe it was the first signs of menopause. Or maybe it was that June was now a senior in high school.

Or maybe, just maybe, it was the little slut she'd found her husband screwing that August.

Well, whatever the reason, when the holidays rolled around Sheila began having a harder and harder time holding it all together. And soon, though she tried hard to hide it, all she could think about was how to get back at the bastard.

In August, when she had caught the idiot, though, Sheila didn't even let on she was angry. Nope. She had no problem keeping her cool then. She didn't even raise her voice.

"Really, Walter?"

That was the first thing she said. Okay, maybe the tone was patronizing, but it was still calm. "*Really?* After all these years?"

She looked up and down the length of the little thing hiding her body under the sheets, under *her* sheets.

"You at least could have had better taste."

Better taste might not have been the kindest thing to say, but under the circumstances, she still demonstrated impressive restraint.

After that, Sheila left the room. Then she left the house. She didn't even slam the door. No, thinking back about it later, Sheila was proud of how smoothly and noiselessly she had closed those doors.

Not wanting to give Walter the satisfaction of thinking she cared, Sheila simply wrote him off. In the weeks that followed, she cleaned out his drawers, stuffing some of his shit in garbage bags and packing the rest away in the attic. After that, she filed for divorce. Wiped her hands of him. End of a goddamn era.

Sheila ultimately got the house, custody of June, who was about to turn eighteen anyway, and a big enough settlement that she probably would be able to quit her job at the garden center.

Of course, it was hard on June at first. Naturally, the girl resented her father.

"It's something you'll learn about men one day, if you don't know it already," Sheila told her daughter. "With maybe a couple exceptions, they're self-consumed, stature-crazed, sex-obsessed animals. You can't take these things personally."

Perhaps it wasn't the most optimistic speech, but June told her mom that in general she seemed remarkably Zen about it all.

"Mom, you're, like, remarkably Zen about this whole thing."

"This whole thing?"

"You know, Dad sleeping with that whore."

"June!"

"Well? What do you want me to call her?"

"How about we don't call her anything, okay?"

June exhaled loudly and looked away.

"Besides," Sheila went on, "this *whole thing,* as you call it, may end up being the best thing that happened to me, to us. Just got to keep it all in perspective."

"That's what I'm trying to say, Mom. You're doing good." She took a Diet Coke from the fridge. "But she's still a whore."

THERE WAS GOOD REASON for Sheila to be proud, at least for a time. Life returned to a kind of normal. Better than normal in some ways. She suddenly had all this free time. She had more time to spend with June. She had more time to go to the dojo, where she was only weeks away from earning her purple belt. And she had more time to work on her art.

Indeed, until December, life was pretty good. But then her divorce became official, and all the stores started blaring Christmas carols, and something began to change. Sheila couldn't get Walter out of her head. She started having these bouts of rage. And she secretly started scheming ways to come at that lying cheat with a ten-plagues-style attack.

Sheila began driving a lot faster. She would slam on her brakes when pedestrians entered the crosswalk. She glared at them, like it was their fault. She leaned on her horn.

It was a strange sight to see. Sheila drove an art car, decorated bumper to bumper with bunnies. Ordinarily, drivers of art cars don't speed and honk.

"Mom! Those are little kids crossing the street. They didn't do anything wrong!"

Sheila wouldn't hear it. She mumbled more and more about other cars on the road or about how long it was taking for the "piece-of-shit light" to change. She rarely abided by the rules at four-way stops, often jumping into the intersection first and then throwing her hands up at the other drivers when they honked at her.

Yes, driving was definitely the first indication that all was not well. But the first real incident occurred in January at a protest on campus. Sheila went to a lot of these rallies. Rallies against the war. Against guns. Against fracking. Against the Citizens United decision.

She had even started a Facebook group called *We Don't Rest, We Protest*. The members were mainly former hippies who got equally outraged about similar issues. On corners, they held up banners with painted slogans. Cars would pass and honk. Sometimes petitions were circulated. Sometimes they collected donations. But mostly they just held up signs. Of course, Sheila recycled the materials as much as possible, pasting over the old slogans or writing on the back of the poster board for different causes.

This particular rally was against the Israeli occupation of the West Bank. When the group decided to break for lunch, Sheila put her sign down. And that's when she realized what she'd done.

"Shit, shit, shit, shit," she said under her breath. And then a little louder, "Ah, Sheila! Don't tell me I was…"

Well she was. All day, Sheila had been holding up the wrong side of the board. Among all the various slogans urging a free Palestine, Sheila had been vigorously waiving a sign that read, "Corporations are NOT People!"

It wasn't really that big a deal. Ordinarily she would have just laughed. But on that particular day, Sheila didn't laugh. She felt like a complete fool and went red with embarrassment. The embarrassment turned into anger, an anger so frightening and unfamiliar that she didn't know how to contain it.

She thought of Walter then. Her instinct was still to blame him when anything went wrong, to trace some circuitous logical path back to that stupid man and his infidelity.

When she realized Walter couldn't be blamed, she set to ripping apart the poster. This was awkward and difficult given that the board was thick and hard to tear. Eventually, she just folded it in half and threw the damn thing to the ground. She stomped on it like a child.

One kid with long hair tied up under a Rasta cap said, "Whoa, dude. Check her out!"

"Whoa yourself, asshole!" Her pulse was racing. "Why the hell didn't you say something?"

He looked at her incredulously. "About what?"

"*About what?* About that my sign was backwards all day is what!"

He didn't know what she was talking about and said so, trying not to laugh.

"Oh, sure. Sure you didn't know." She scanned the group of students who had gathered. "You all knew. You feel so righteous, don't you? Holding your little signs."

Sheila started screaming. "But you're as bad as they are, those settlers over there, aren't you? You don't really give a shit about anyone but yourselves and your little worlds."

"Holy. Hang on lady." The kid spoke slowly, excessively calm, something he had probably learned in a debate class. "I don't even know what you're talking about. But look, none of us knew about your sign, or we would have just told you to spin it around. Chill."

"Chill?"

"For real. Who cares?"

"*Who cares?* If you don't care, why the heck are you out here?"

"What the hell, lady? That's not what I meant."

"Don't be an asshole."

"You're the one being an asshole. It's really not that big a deal." The guy waived the back of his hand at her and turned away.

Sheila felt her cheeks get hot, and her vision blurred. Her jaw ached from grinding her teeth. She tasted bile in her mouth. It made her think a migraine might be coming on, or that she might vomit.

"Fuck you," she yelled through tightened lips. But the crowd was dispersing. He was well out of hearing range.

Clusters of kids went off in various directions. Sheila stood there alone and tried to breathe. God, she hated Walter then. *Probably wouldn't have even been out here in the first place,* she thought, *if that piece of shit could have kept his dick in his pants.*

She grabbed her jacket and her bag and went toward her car. Her hands were shaking as she tried to unlock the door. She dropped the keys. When she finally got in, she rested her head against the steering wheel and struggled not to cry.

❖

THE SECOND BIG OUTBURST came in March. Sheila was what some might call an *outsider artist.* She made sculptures in her free time. It was something Walter had always encouraged, she had to admit. Her pieces were conceptual, made primarily of flotsam and jetsam that she collected on the shore or on the side of the road—car parts, old buoys, driftwood.

Her friends called it *found art.* The term had never bothered her before. She even used it herself from time to time. But apparently that time had passed. And one morning Sheila snapped.

A neighbor walking a dog saw she was working on something and tried to be friendly. "I'm a big fan of found art." That was all he said. His tone was pleasant enough.

Sheila whipped around from the large piece of foam she was spray-painting and gave him a withering look. "It's not found *art,* you moron. I don't *find* the art! I *make* it. I find the *materials.* I do *not* find the art."

June was sitting on the porch. She came running down toward the curb. "Sorry about her," she said. Then in a whisper, "What the hell, Mom?"

"Well, June," her tone was syrupy, "do *you* think someone could just find something like this lying around? It's insulting. It's…it's unintelligent."

The man was still standing there. He heard every word, so June apologized again. He turned and walked off, shaking his head.

"That was, like, pretty crazy, mom. The guy did nothing wrong. Who cares what somebody calls it?"

There it was again. The apathy of the young. Sheila hollered at her daughter. "*Who cares?* What's with you kids? I care!"

Sheila held up the piece she was making, suddenly eyeing it critically.

"It's *conceptual* art, June. That's what it is. I am a conceptual artist, and that is what it should be called. *Conceptual.* You can't find a piece like this just sitting around. For Christ's sake."

Later that afternoon, Sheila was working on the same hunk of foam when the mailman came with her mail.

"What is that, some sort of creature?"

The look Sheila shot him made him intuitively clutch his saddlebag tighter. But it didn't stop him from hazarding a guess.

"Armadillo?"

Her glare intensified.

"Beaver?"

No one ever knew what Sheila's sculptures were. Never bothered her before. But that was the old Sheila.

"You blind?" she barked. "Use your eyes!"

"Porcupine?" he tried again.

"What's with you men? You're all fools. It's a bridge!" Sheila looked at it again. She hesitated a moment, but then she said it again. "It's a damn bridge."

"A *bridge*?" He sounded doubtful.

She mocked his tone. "A *porcupine*?"

"Well, it…"

"Well, it what? Do you even know what a porcupine looks like?"

"Apparently not," he said, dropping her mail hard on the step and then walking off. "But I sure as shit know what a bridge looks like."

IN RETROSPECT, THAT EXCHANGE was the tipping point, when Sheila's rage shifted from isolated outbursts to a more constant state of frustration and anger. And then in early summer, the car thing happened.

Maybe ten years earlier, still apparently happily married, Sheila got an idea. After a friend painted zebra stripes on her white Taurus and another acquaintance turned the roof of his Volvo wagon into an Astroturf field, complete with fake flowers and a foot-tall grazing clay goat, Sheila decided to turn the family's white VW Bug into what they came to call "Bug's Bunnies."

With some industrial-strength epoxy, Sheila affixed a coat of faux fur to every inch of the car's exterior, then glued little rabbits all over the dash. With the help of some orange fabric, the antenna became a carrot. She formed a tail by attaching a poof of cotton to the hatchback. She even fashioned two floppy ears out of coat hangers and white and pink felt.

For a long time, she loved the car. Walter loved it. June loved it. June's friends loved it. Everyone loved it. It was a great conversation piece. People would stop and point, take pictures. It even got written up in the local paper. Sheila kept the clipping on the fridge for years.

But when this wave of aggression came, Sheila started to feel self-conscious about the car. "Oh, hell," she'd say beneath her breath when people clustered around it snapping photos. "Not again."

Returning to the car after running errands started to feel as if she were leaving a courtroom after a guilty verdict. People were always asking her how she did it, what inspired it, trying to get a closer look, wanting to get into her space, nosing around her business.

She started shooing people away. Even children. "Get away from the car," she'd yell. "Get your hands off it! You're getting the fur dirty. How would you like it if I touched your car, huh? If I took pictures of your back seat?"

She came to believe people were whispering about her and her car, even when the car was nowhere in sight. She saw people miming bunny ears, faking an overbite, hopping around and pointing at her.

"That's the bunny lady," she'd hear. "What's up, doc?"

And then, in late June, under a perfectly blue sky, a driver gave Sheila the finger for cutting him off on the freeway. He mouthed some expletive. Sheila thought he called her a "bunny killer."

She raced home recklessly, parked the car half up on the curb and jumped out. Then she just went at it. Sheila tore off every bunny she could. She ripped off that dumb tail. She bent the orange antenna back and forth until it snapped. She clawed at the fur, tugging at it, grunting as she yanked. Where the glue was too strong, she used a flathead and a hammer, wedging the screwdriver in and then prying off the biggest pieces she could. And all the time she was ranting about Walter, about *kids today*, about wanting to burn down everything around her. "Just burn it all," she was saying. "The house. The town. The hills. What the hell do I care anymore?"

She hardly stopped to look up. When she did pause for a moment to catch her breath, she saw her big-bearded neighbor looking at her through his bay window. For several months he had just been peering out that window most of every day.

"Whatcha staring at, you weirdo?"

She tried to shoo him away. He eventually disappeared, and Sheila returned to the car.

It took well over an hour, but she managed to get most of the fur off. The car looked terrible, like it had been dragged on its sides down the Interstate. The screwdriver had left scrapes and dents all over. Most of the paint was chipped off. Some patches of fur remained. Glue residue was everywhere.

"Oh my God, Mom!" June shrieked when she came home and saw the damage.

Sheila wiped her brow.

"What happened?"

Sheila raised her eyebrows.

"Oh my God!"

Sheila still said nothing.

"What the hell happened? Who did this? Did you do this? Why did you do this?"

Sheila wiped her brow and started walking off toward the house. "Are you hungry?" she asked her daughter, still walking away. "I'm starving. Want to go get something to eat?"

"What? Am I *hungry*? No! Tell me, what's going on?"

"How about Chinese?"

"Mom! Look at our car!"

"How about let's not mention it, okay?"

"Not mention it?"

Sheila opened her front door and went into her room. She closed the door quietly but firmly. June looked again at the destroyed car and then ran into the house. She banged on her mother's door. Asked again what could possibly have gotten into her.

Through the wood, Sheila finally offered a sighing "I don't know, June. I guess I just give up."

June opened the door slowly. She flopped beside her mother on the bed. They lay silently for a while staring at some peeling paint on the ceiling.

"Think maybe you should, like, I don't know, talk to someone?"

"You mean like a shrink?" Sheila laughed. "Jesus. Don't be silly."

"Well, you got to talk to someone, Mom."

Sheila closed her eyes.

"How about Dad, then? Maybe it's time to go talk to Dad."

Sheila bolted upright, eyes wide. "Not on your life."

"No, really. Like, yell at him. Curse at him. I don't know. Hit him. You gotta do something."

"No chance. I wouldn't give him the satisfaction…" She trailed off. Looked out the window. Then she hugged her arms to her chest. "Oh June," she said after a time. "I thought I had put all the crap behind me."

"Me, too. But, Jesus, it doesn't look like…"

"But listen. One thing I am *not* doing is seeing your father. That I'm just not doing."

June lay there, resting her head against her mother's shoulder. "How about we go away?" she asked cautiously. "A mother-daughter weekend, you know?"

Sheila shook her head.

"A spa? There's this great one I heard about where you sit in tubs of hot mulch. Doesn't that sound amazing?"

Sheila looked down at June. "Hot mulch? No. It certainly does not sound amazing. It sounds disgusting. Listen, I don't need to go anywhere. I just need a little time to myself. I'll be fine. I am fine."

"Sorry, Mom, but you are *not* fine."

"Okay. Enough. Enough. Tell me about school today, honey."

"Mom!"

"What's new with what's his name?"

"His name's Pete. Who cares about Pete?! Look at our car! I can't be seen in that!"

Sheila looked out the window. Then she collapsed back onto the bed. "It'll pass, June. It always does."

"How about camping? A shopping spree? The beach? A makeover?"

Sheila shook her head at them all. Finally, June suggested they have a yard sale, that they clean out the attic and get rid of all her dad's junk that was still up there.

Sheila finally didn't veto it. So June suggested they do it that very Saturday. "Come on, Mom. It'll be fun."

Perhaps out of fatigue, Sheila agreed.

"Okay!" June said, relieved. "Saturday it is. And maybe then we can use the money we make for facials."

❖

THAT FRIDAY, HOWEVER, WHEN June got home from school, her father's bowling ball, golf clubs, a box of records, and bags of clothes were already out on the curb. Sheila had also brought down a few of her sculptures.

June saw her mom coming out of the house lugging another one toward the street. "Got a head start, eh Mom?"

"What's that, sweetie?"

June caught up with her. "I said you started without me. We said Saturday. What's up with that?"

"Oh, well, what difference does it make? There's still plenty to do. Come on, grab an end." Sheila told June that she was feeling better already, that this was a good idea.

"Your art, too, though? What are you doing with that?"

The tin man Sheila had crafted out of an old muffler was out there. The bridge the mailman mistook for a porcupine was out there.

"Figured I might as well get rid of it all. Don't you think?"

June didn't answer.

Sheila was hauling out something that looked vaguely like the Eiffel Tower. June couldn't figure out where to grab to help carry it.

"It's just…Mom, you worked so hard on these."

"Not really. And I can always make more."

A gray brontosaurus came next.

"Really, Mom? Even our old dinosaur? I like him."

"*Like him*? June, you haven't seen him in years. None of us have."

"But…"

Sheila stopped and set the brontosaurus down. She wiped a few strands of gray hair off her brow. "But what, June? Who am I kidding?"

"What are you talking about?"

"Look. Nobody likes the crap I make. It's not like I don't know."

"That's not true."

"Yes, it is."

"But, Mom, did you see that YouTube video about that musician guy who made all that music by recording wind and animals and things?"

"What? No, I certainly did not. Your point?"

"Nobody ever got his stuff, but he kept doing it. Then Scion or something heard it, and now he's, like, all over the place."

"That's not going to happen to me." Sheila shrugged her shoulders. "I don't even care."

For the rest of the afternoon, Sheila sat out on the curb. And she was still sitting there after it got dark. Nothing sold. June watched from the kitchen window. When people walked by without even looking at the stuff on the tables, Sheila stared them down, sometimes even called after them. The plan appeared to be backfiring. If anything, she appeared to be getting angrier.

"Don't get down, Mom. You can't, like, get discouraged. I've never heard of someone putting stuff out on a Friday before. That was crazy. Tomorrow's the big day. I'll be with you."

So all day Saturday, she and June stood out there. And June was right. People came. Her husband's stuff went. Most of it, anyway. Of course, that was largely because of how Sheila priced his things. A buck for the bowling ball. Five dollars for a decent set of golf clubs. A quarter a record. It felt so good. Sheila got great satisfaction selling his prized possessions for pennies.

"You like it? Just take the stupid thing," she would say if someone was eyeing one of his blazers or some of his camping gear. "Otherwise, I'm going to burn it all anyway." People would look up in alarm, and Sheila would smile like she was kidding. But she wasn't really kidding.

Some of June's old clothes and toys were down there as well. Most of that sold. But no one showed even the slightest interest in the sculptures. And as the day dragged on, Sheila began getting depressed again. By the time they called it quits, Sheila was a wreck.

Early Sunday morning, June rolled over and looked out the window. Her mom was already out there. "Ah, fuck," June said, pulling herself out of bed to put water on for tea. She pulled jeans on and went down with two cups to ask how she was doing.

"Good. Better. A lot better. I have a good feeling about today."

June stayed for a couple hours and kept her mother company.

A few people came and rifled through a remaining box of books, eyed the rack of ties and dress shirts. A pickup cruised by slowly. The driver asked if Sheila was selling any scrap metal. The young woman who worked at the library stopped in and bought one of June's old Halloween costumes. A family walked over from across the street and took June's first bicycle.

Around noon, it started to get real quiet. Sheila sighed. June went back inside. Sheila began to admit that no one else was likely to come and started to pack things up.

But then, as she was stuffing some of Walter's clothes back into a garbage bag, Sheila noticed a woman approaching. She had a shy, sweet smile and wore a loose-fitting wool sweater with a felt poodle on it. Her hair was light brown and needed a wash. Sheila could see that she was very thin. Too thin. *Maybe the sweater used to fit*, Sheila thought. Still, she was very pretty, with big, deep gray eyes that looked wounded.

"These are amazing," she said in a fragile voice.

"What?" Sheila's tone was too aggressive, almost defensive, and the woman recoiled slightly.

"They're amazing," she repeated.

"I heard you," Sheila said a little more kindly. "Just didn't know what you were referring to."

"These," the lady said, pointing to the sculptures.

"Those?"

"Where'd you get them all?"

"Where? From the garage mostly," she laughed.

The woman looked confused.

"I made them!"

"No!"

"Yes."

"No!"

Sheila smiled.

"You're serious?"

"Every one of them."

"They're amazing. Did I already say that?"

"You did." Sheila began to enjoy the interaction. "But I don't mind hearing it again. Most people think they're crap."

The lady shook her head and walked around the table. "What a cool bridge."

"You knew it was a bridge?" Sheila softened even more.

"What else could it be?"

"Some guy thought it was a porcupine."

"Some guys are assholes."

Sheila laughed at that, maybe a little too hard. "That's more or less what I told him."

The woman didn't say anything for a while. Then she added, "Sometimes I want to tell that to my husband, too."

Sheila wasn't sure what to say to that. She was about to blurt out something about Walter and his little affair, but the woman saved her by speaking again.

"I wish I had half your talent. You're lucky."

Sheila blushed. "You're kind. Haven't been feeling so lucky lately." Their eyes met for a moment. The younger woman nodded, knowingly.

"And that dinosaur? Oh, I just love that dinosaur."

Sheila tilted her head and squinted in slight disbelief.

"You didn't make that, did you?"

"I did. That's an old one, actually. I started out in a more, I guess, literal style."

The lady smiled. "She's beautiful. Is it a she?"

That made Sheila laugh. "Well, not that literal, I guess. Don't know. We used to call him Barry. So I guess we thought it was a he."

"Looks like a she to me. More like a Thelma. Look at the eyes. Definitely a she. How'd you make her? Did you use some kind of mold or a kit?"

"Nope. Freehand."

"No!"

Sheila tried to match her enthusiasm. "Yes!"

"Amazing."

"It's just Styrofoam. I find it all down by the water or behind the big box stores. I glued some pieces together until I had a big, odd-shaped block. Then I used this sculpting tool I have. It gets hot, and you can slice through almost anything. Of course, I used finer knives to do the details."

"Of course."

The woman paused like she was considering something. There was mock orange growing along the driveway, and Sheila watched as this strange woman took a deep breath and then smiled.

"How much you want for her?"

"What do you mean?"

"What are you selling her for?"

"You want it?"

"Of course I want it."

Sheila went quiet for a minute. "Take it," she said suddenly.

"What do you mean take it?"

"I mean, just take it. Please. It's yours."

"Please let me pay you something for it."

"No, really," Sheila said with a smile. "It means a lot that you like it."

"But I insist."

"No. *I insist.* Really. Just give him a good home."

The woman paused. She looked at her shoes and then said, slightly to herself, "I'll try my best." Then she sighed, looked back up and smiled. "Thank you, um…"

"Sheila."

"Thank you, Sheila. So much. I'm Martha."

Sheila held her hand out awkwardly. Martha ignored it and went in for a hug. "You made my day."

Sheila loosened from the slightly uncomfortable embrace. "Mine, too, Martha. Really."

Martha ran her hand gently along the back of the dinosaur's neck and then lifted it off the table carefully, holding it in her arms like it was a baby.

Sheila was a little taken aback by the tenderness with which Martha held it, not necessarily appropriate for a fake brontosaurus covered in dust.

Martha turned back after a few houses and waived. For a moment she looked to be as young as June.

Sheila looked down at her table of sculptures. June had been watching the scene through the living room window and came out.

"Did that lady just buy the dinosaur?"

"Well, not exactly."

"Not exactly?"

"I gave it to her."

"You did?"

"She liked it so much, I just gave it to her."

June looked at her mother. "You okay, Mom?"

Sheila thought about it for a minute. She looked at her daughter. She looked at the table of her work. "You know, June," she said after a while. "I think I am."

"Are you sure?"

"Yes, I think I'm fine. In fact, I think I just got an idea for a new piece."

❖

A FEW WEEKS AFTER the yard sale, Sheila told June that she had almost finished her new creation.

"Can I see it?"

"Not yet. But it's going to be a real whopper."

June's look showed some concern. "It's not a burger, is it?" Sheila just smiled but didn't say.

The next night, while June was up in her room, Sheila hollered that she was going out for a little bit. She put on black pants and a tight black top. She hadn't completely lost her figure. She put on dark eye shadow and lipstick for the first time in months. Then she tied the new sculpture to the roof of her still-messed-up car and screeched out of the driveway.

June woke up when she heard her mother come back in the house a few hours later. She came down the stairs sleepily and saw her at the table having a glass of red wine. Her face looked flushed, but relaxed. She looked great actually, and June said so. Then June looked at her mother's fingernails and the legs of her pants.

"What the hell, Mom? You're covered in mud! Where have you been?"

Sheila took a long sip of wine and looked at her daughter. "Your father's," she announced with a triumphant smile.

"Dad's?"

"Yep."

"Were you wrestling?"

Sheila laughed.

"Well, were you?"

"No! We were definitely not wrestling."

"Well?"

"Well what?"

"Come on, Mom. What happened?"

"Not sure there's so much to say," Sheila told her, topping off her glass. Her words were measured, and her voice was quiet.

"Stop being like this. There's got to be stuff to say. What did you tell him? How'd he take it? What happened?"

"He didn't say anything. I didn't either."

"Jesus, Mom, what are you talking about?"

"I didn't see him."

June squinted in confusion.

"Look, how about we talk about it tomorrow? It's late. I didn't really go to see him. I had a job to do, and I did it."

SHEILA WOKE EARLY THE next morning. She made tea and went out on the front porch to drink it. That's where Walter used to take his coffee and where she imagined he would have it at his new place. She wanted to picture exactly what his morning would be like, wanted to go through similar motions.

She sipped from her mug and looked out over the dew-soaked flowerbed as the sun rose over the hills. She smelled mint growing. It wouldn't be too long before the plums on the tree in her yard ripened.

A few miles away, Walter groggily opened the door. He'd had too much vodka the night before. He stepped outside, took a slow sip of coffee from his mug, looked up and then spit the hot liquid all over his steps.

In the middle of his lawn, dug in deep so it would take some effort to remove, was a sculpture. It was easily six-feet high and four-feet wide. The core was wire and foam, and it was covered entirely with pieces of Walter's crap that hadn't sold: strips of his tweed coats, cuff links, broken pieces of his old records, even some baseball cards, which were probably worth something. It stood like a totem, casting a long shadow. There, in the middle of Walter's well-groomed front lawn, was a huge hand, its large and vaguely phallic middle finger standing up tall and proud, for all the world to see.

DRIFTWOOD

PLAINVIEW WAS HARVEY'S LAST hope. He'd heard there might be union work at the deep-water port and that even someone his age and in his condition might get hired. So he took the Greyhound down from Idaho, a twenty-five-hour trip. Thanks to a screaming baby and a dirty bathroom, Harvey hardly slept. It was 7:00 a.m. when the bus finally arrived. His eyes were red, his shirt stained. He bought a cup of coffee at the station and then made his way down to the docks.

Every gig Harvey ever held was on, or at least near, water. He dropped out of high school in '72 and hitchhiked his way to St. Lawrence. Worked the locks for a couple of years. From there, he joined the Merchant Marine and sailed all over the world. He worked in the engine room on a cargo ship that did the China-to-Los Angeles route several times a year. Then he became a river guide. The Snake and the Salmon, primarily. In his late forties, the company wanted younger guides, so Harvey moved down to the Keys and took tourists on charter fishing trips out of Key Largo. Resurrection Bay, Alaska, was next. Got a grueling job as a longline fisherman. That was the hardest job he'd had, and it took a lot of bourbon to make it through. At the end of his second season, he busted his right leg in an accident that probably should have killed him.

So he went back to Idaho, back to his childhood home. He needed time for his leg to heal, which it never fully did. He also wanted to be there to help his ailing father die. They hadn't talked much in decades, and Harvey wanted to make peace before it was too late. Harvey was good to him in the end. He reminded his father of all the things he'd taught him when he was younger, how to read water, how to gauge the current, estimate depths, learn from a coastline. His dad had taught Harvey how to tie a fly, where to wade, how to wait. He also taught him how to whittle, which apart from drinking was just about the only thing Harvey did in his free time.

"You taught me all I know about wood. Wood and water. Jesus, Dad, that's quite a gift for a father to give a son."

If asked, the guys he'd worked with over the years likely would have recalled that, for a big guy who had worked just about every day of his adult life, Harvey had real soft hands. And that those hands almost always held a piece of driftwood and a big pocketknife. It was an aberration in his otherwise rough and weathered persona, how gently and patiently he worked his blade along the grain, that he could turn old and overlooked pieces of burl into buffalo, snakes, heron, canyon wrens. His creations had grace, elegance. They were detailed, too, often possessing surprising emotion in the contours of their carved faces.

✤

WHEN HARVEY LIMPED OFF the Greyhound, he looked like he'd stepped out of a sea shanty or stumbled out of the great North Woods. His cargo pants were paint-stained. His leathery face was covered in stubble. It had been four days since his last shower, and his silver hair showed it. From years under the sun, Harvey's skin was dark, his lips permanently cracked.

He landed the job on the spot, duffel bag still slung over his shoulder. Semiskilled laborer. It was far below Harvey's experience level and pay grade. But it was a job, and he wasn't exactly in a place to be choosy. The work would primarily involve various maintenance projects, equipment upkeep, painting and patching, road repair. None of that would be a problem for Harvey.

During breaks, Harvey watched as the big container ships coming in from China were unloaded. Maersk Lines, COSCO, OOCL. Much of what came in was computer parts for cars and cellphones.

Harvey came of age in an era when cars didn't have computers and telephones weren't smart. He didn't know the first thing about tech. Didn't even own a cell phone.

"The ships, I still get," Harvey said to a guy working next to him. "It's what they're carrying nowadays I can't understand. The fuck is it all for?"

The work itself wasn't the problem. If anything, it was too easy. And too much of it was on dry land. His mind was never on the task at hand. He'd miss frayed belts, split timbers. Came close to cutting off his coworker's arm with a chainsaw.

The foreman would catch him staring out at the watery horizon. Harvey watched the younger kids on the decks of the ships, their whole lives ahead of them. He saw them coming into port, saw the ships set sail. He cursed them all under his breath. Harvey wasn't meant to stay on shore. But he knew that at his age no one was going to take him out on a rig.

When he wasn't at work, Harvey bounced around between the park, the marina, the library. He sat in the window of the donut shop and drank weak coffee out of Styrofoam cups. He watched the spin cycle at the Laundromat. He rode the all-night city buses, just to see where he'd end up. Then he'd try to find his way back home. He got in a few fights. He made no real friends.

What difference did it make to some kid with a mustache and a fancy laptop that Harvey could tie a trucker's hitch in the rain while balancing atop a load? Did the goth librarian care that he could haul in a ninety-pound halibut, could navigate a Class V rapid, had steered ships through archipelagos, could start a fire if need be without a match. What did it matter in the city how a river snaked its way through the country, how it bore into the rock, how it formed a canyon over the centuries? Who wanted to hear him describe how a storm formed out over the open seas, how it could transform a placid surface into furious, spitting volcanoes faster than a college kid in tight jeans could hand-drip one of those fancy coffees?

Pretty soon, Harvey was drinking heavily again. At first, it was just at a bar down by the water. But, before long, he was tucking a Coke bottle of bourbon into his coat pocket on the way to work, and he'd pull from it behind the gears of his backhoe whenever he had the chance. It was only a matter of time before the boss smelled it on his clothes and breath.

Harvey knew the foreman didn't like him. But when the guy noticed the booze, a line was crossed. He sent

Harvey home and told him not to come back until he was sober. Put him on a kind of probation, until he'd proved himself reliable again. Harvey was lucky that he even was granted a second chance. But, of course, he didn't see it that way. Harvey didn't take well to someone half his age giving him a hard time. He said as much and added a few other pleasantries as he walked off. The boss heard. And that was that.

After only a few months, Harvey was out of work again. He didn't know what to do. Without a job or anything keeping him in a city he was never attached to in the first place, he decided to return to Idaho. Since his father had passed, his old house stood empty. He could stay there until he figured out his next move.

So Harvey packed his bag again and headed back to the Greyhound station. An enormous moon was just coming up over the hills when Harvey crossed the street. The last time he recalled seeing a moon that big was over the Indian Ocean, and he took it as a good sign that he was making the right decision.

That big moon calmed him, gave him hope. It felt good to be on the move. Good enough that he figured he could get a drink before catching his bus. A toast to getting fired. To saying good riddance to Plainview. A toast to setting sail again.

The Anchor had no windows and no sign out front, save a flickering neon martini glass. As far as Harvey could tell, the place never closed. He didn't know many of the regulars' actual names, but he knew their faces. Most of the guys were other dockworkers and deckhands. Some were there nightly. Some came in every few months when their ships came in. He knew their stories. Knew whose wife had left him, who was out of work, whose kid had been a star point guard, who had a gambling problem.

Harvey was relaxed in there. He opened up more. Didn't feel judged. Something in the way stories got told over that old mahogany slab of wood and bottles of beer reminded him a little of the way folks talked out at sea.

"What's in the sack, captain?" someone asked Harvey after the door shut behind him.

"Time to pack it in, Skates."

"Yeah?" Someone else asked.

"Setting sail."

The guys knew not to ask why.

"Gave them my notice," Harvey told them. "Well, if you call this notice." He flipped off the TV monitor in the corner.

"Son of a bitch."

"Son of a bitch is right." He motioned for a drink. "Wasn't the first time. Probably won't be the last."

"Where to now?"

"Back home, I suppose."

"Home?"

"Idaho."

"Whereabouts?" the bartender asked, handing Harvey a tall pour of Wild Turkey. "On the house," he added.

Harvey raised the glass in acknowledgment and swallowed half the drink. "Gracias." He exhaled long. "Up near Lewiston, where the Snake runs through." Another generous pour arrived. "Yeah, there's a Potlach plant up there. Maybe they'll be hiring."

A ball game was on, and a few of the guys were looking up at the screen in the corner talking about some drug scandal. Harvey emptied that glass, too. He began talking.

"I was born on a river, you know." No one said anything, but they all heard. "The Snake. Hell's Canyon. Ever been?"

He figured no one had, though one guy seemed to nod.

"Big river, you know. Deep, deep canyon. Deepest gorge in North America."

"What about the Grand?"

"Hell's is deeper."

"No way."

"Ma went into labor a few weeks early," Harvey continued, ignoring the comment. "Even still, my dad and her were three days in and at least one away from anything resembling a road. Not sure why they were out there in the first place that late in the whole process."

Some guy who always spoke in clichés said, "Things were different back then."

"I'll say," someone added, perhaps sarcastically.

"Dad was at the oars, of course. And they said that when I was ready to come, I was ready to come. No time to go for help. Not sure where he'd have got to, anyhow. Hell, there was barely time to get to shore."

The story was a true one, or at least he'd come to believe it as true. And Harvey told it well. He told them about the rapids his father had navigated as he tried to get to shore, about his mother screaming and cursing at him from the floor of the bouncing boat to "keep it steady," to "take it easy," then to "hurry the hell up," and then a whole string of cuss words.

"Finally, Dad managed to get to a flat spot where he could pull the boat into an eddy and then up onto shore." Harvey tapped his empty glass against the dark wood. "I've been back to that little beach a number of times."

A guy a few stools down bought another round, and Harvey poured it down his throat.

"Dad tied the boat to a rock as quick as he could and then ran around trying to figure out how to clear an area for me to come. He set to gathering wood to make a fire. I suppose he'd heard something about needing hot water and a lot of rags. So while he was collecting twigs and branches, he also started pulling off his clothes—his shirt, his pants, everything—started ripping them apart. Just tore up all his clothes. He was quite a sight, running around showing it all to the heavens, trying to start a fire."

There was laughter. Another bourbon soon appeared.

"Meantime, Ma is still in the boat—and I'm, of course, still in my Ma. The boat's half up onto shore. She's just groaning and whaling, 'Baby's coming, my baby's coming, sweet Jesus, my baby's coming!'

"Dad's shouting, too: 'Hang on, hang on, I'll have it all ready in a minute. Just hang on!' He's clearing away rocks and sticks from this strip of beach beside the boat. He's blowing and fanning the kindling, trying to get the fire going. He's cussing and shouting. He's running around in circles.

"Well, as I said, I wasn't waiting for him or for anyone. And just as that fire caught, I came shooting out into the bottom of the boat. Blood and river water all mixed up."

"Holy hell," someone said.

Another guy breathed a "Christ."

The bartender topped Harvey's glass and poured a couple fingers for himself. He leaned back against the shelves of drinks and smiled. Harvey took a big swallow.

"So then dad, naked still, jumps back into the boat. He scooped me up off the bottom and cut the cord. With his hunting knife, he cut it. How many can say came into the world that way? Cord cut by a Bowie? Dad tried to stop the bleeding with some of those rags he tore. He was scared to high heaven, no doubt. I think he was all of nineteen."

Harvey smiled and nodded slowly. "He probably didn't have a clue in the world what to do next, how to help, or who to hold, me or Ma. I'm sure there was a lot of screaming going on. All three of us, I guess. Well, then Dad did the only thing he knew how to do well. He ran that river."

"What happened to the fire?" someone cut in.

Harvey laughed and finished his drink. "Never thought about that. Left it burning, I suppose. At any rate, he pulled on those oars like he'd never pulled before. We raced downstream, through rapids that probably would've made us scream, had we not already been screaming. Those granite walls are sheer. In places they go up almost a thousand feet. The water was swirling and spitting up into the boat. The canyon wrens were darting this way and that, whistling those falling notes."

Harvey did his best wren impersonation and soon they were all nodding, like they all knew that country well. Another round got purchased and passed.

"I worked on that river when I got older," Harvey continued, slurring more and more, his words spreading out. "It's powerful out there, where the Snake and Salmon meet. That's a holy spot if ever there was one. For the Nez Perce who lived up there. For me, too. In some ways, it's the only place I ever felt at home."

Harvey let the story trail off. No one said anything. Harvey felt like he had shared too much, felt a little ashamed, empty like the glass in front of him. He poured a last dark drop down his throat and stood up. Something tightened up in him as he wound his narrative down, like some door was closing, or rather like he couldn't figure out where the door was to close.

"Yeah, well, I got a lot of that river in me still," he said mostly to himself. "And that's God's truth. I guess that's the point of it all."

Harvey left a fifty-dollar bill on the bar. He didn't have to. The drinks would have been on the house. But he wasn't sure if he'd ever be back, if he'd ever see those guys again. He didn't believe in leaving debts behind.

"Well, don't know how long I'll be gone," he said. "Or if I'll even be coming back this way. So fare thee well, as we used to say." And with that, Harvey grabbed his bag, walked out the door, and headed off toward the station.

❖

IT WAS REALLY LATE, and he was really drunk. Harvey had never been good with time. He didn't make it to the station that night. Got as far as the park around the corner. Must have laid down there in the grass, for that's where he woke up the next morning, his arm around his duffel, like it was a lady.

In the cool shade of the trees, bird sounds all around, Harvey stretched his legs. For a few sweet minutes, he thought he was home, that he had in fact caught that bus, slept the entire ride, and that the city was far, far behind him.

Eyes still closed, he reached out and felt the deep, damp grass under his palms. He breathed in the air of his youth. He could even sense the river somewhere nearby. The Earth was both strong and soft beneath him, just like his backyard growing up. It held him, like he remembered his father used to when he was a kid. Harvey's chest rose and fell, rose and fell, and he took it all in.

"Idaho," he mouthed. "Idaho."

❖

THEN IT HIT HIM. Hard. The buzz, the noise, the rush above it all. It was unmistakable. Electricity in the lines, radio waves in the air, cell phone signals, the Internet beaming every which way, distant highways, trains, all the people.

Harvey felt it first in his hands, like a rope burn. He opened and closed them stiffly. He wasn't in Idaho. Of course he wasn't. He hadn't taken any bus. He hadn't even made it to the station. He slowly opened his stinging eyes. His head throbbed.

"Ah, fuck."

He was still only a few blocks from his place. He lay back and closed his eyes. He took in the noise and the smells. He tried to relax. Tried to breathe deeply. He opened his eyes again, and the clouds began to spin above his head. He shielded his face with his big hands, and then he slammed a fist to the ground.

Lying there like that, Harvey thought about driftwood. Not the beautiful pieces couples pick off the Oregon coast, not the pieces he carved, but the ones everyone left behind.

The ones that piled up on the beach, mixed with sea trash, caught up in rocks. They smelled like rot and dead fish. Washed up. Worn down. Bleached by the sun. Stranded on the wrong shore.

He got up stiffly and went to the bodega and bought a coffee and a pack of Aspirin. He wasn't sure what to do. The obvious choice would have been to just head back to the bus station and catch the next bus. But, in the light of day, he could see more clearly that there was nothing back there for him either.

"Ah, shit, Harvey," he said to no one. "What the fuck you gonna do now?"

He knocked around for a few weeks, money running out. He got drunk a lot. One day, he found a rail car on an old strip of abandoned track. Grass had grown high all around the wheels. Someone had cut the padlock on the back door, and the whole inside of the car was tagged with vulgar drawings, proclamations of love, stupid obscenities. Harvey bought a little food and water and a couple bottles of bourbon. He stuffed some clothes into a shirt for a pillow and found a strip of foam to use as a bed.

Harvey stayed in there for nine days, leaving only to go to the bathroom or to get more supplies. Sleeping in that old car, he imagined he was moving somewhere, that he still stood a chance of waking up in another land, in another life. When he finally came out for good, he looked like all hell, but he felt better.

He went to the Wash And Fold, cleaned his clothes and thumbed through the old newspapers. He spotted an ad that said they were hiring at the new bridge.

Harvey paid for a shower at a truck stop and then went down to the construction headquarters. He found the guy in charge and asked what positions were open. Harvey's hair was below his shoulders, and the creases in his face were deep. The boss looked at him skeptically.

"Listen," Harvey told him. "I can do anything you need. I've fixed a turbine generator on a vessel bigger than this whole goddamn span. And that was in thirty-foot swells. I've probably crossed the Pacific more times than you've crossed this puddle. Tell me what you need. I can do it."

The fog was just breaking apart, but it was still cold. The man had some kind of fuzzy headband to keep his ears warm under his hard hat, and Harvey thought no one would have been caught dead wearing something like that back in Alaska or anywhere else he'd worked. They stood around for an awkward while, the guy not saying anything.

"Not sure I like your attitude," the foreman said eventually.

Harvey clenched his fists, but he held the man's gaze and didn't try to argue.

The guy looked Harvey up and down, perhaps trying to determine if Harvey could be counted on. Or maybe he was just asserting his authority by making Harvey wait.

Harvey felt the scrutiny, tried hard not to look away. "Please," Harvey said, eventually. "I need the job."

Another long silence. But then the guy said, "Okay."

Relieved, Harvey shook his hand. "Won't let you down."

"Here's what I'm gonna need from you."

The boss explained that Harvey was to work on a crew of three who would check on and, if need be, tighten the bolts on a section below the roadbed. Once again, he had to swallow his pride and work alongside boys almost a third his age. But it turned out to be pretty good work for him. He was harnessed into scaffolding almost all the time, suspended over the water. His busted leg didn't slow him down, and he could smell the salt water and watch the boats.

Harvey worked hard, and for a while that felt okay. He'd roll an American Spirit on his walk home and smoke it with the satisfaction that he had earned it, that he deserved it.

He found a new apartment down Sacramento. Nothing special. It was a studio on the ground floor of a four-story building with peeling, gray paint. Harvey didn't have any furniture to put in it. He slept right on the carpet.

And Harvey started whittling again. One evening, he found a piece of burl after work and brought it home. He sat out on his stoop under the streetlight and began to carve a hummingbird. An orange trumpet vine grew all over the fence next to his building, and Harvey had watched the hummingbirds dart in and out of it.

He was rusty, though, and his blade wasn't sharp enough. As Harvey was working on that long beak, his knife slipped and sliced into his thumb. He yowled in pain. The blade went in deep, and his thumb started to bleed. Harvey sucked on the wound.

"Son of a…"

He tied a rag around the cut, held it up over his head and went inside to clean it up. Hoping someone had left some Band-Aids behind, Harvey went to the medicine cabinet. Empty. He opened a can of beer instead and took a fistful of aspirin. He replaced the bloody rag with a clean one, had another beer and went to bed.

The next morning was his day off. He headed to the drugstore for a proper bandage. He limped across the park, cradling his thumb. Only a few dog walkers were out and a couple of nannies pushing strollers.

Up ahead, beneath a copse of eucalyptus, he saw a woman sitting with her back to him. It was more or less where he had passed out months before. She was on a checkered blanket, and as he got closer, he saw she was painting. Bright watercolors on small squares of thick, white paper.

He continued toward her. She was painting a bird, some sort of stick coming down out of its belly. *Strange*, he thought, squinting to see it more clearly. *A bird on a spit? A weathervane? A stake? A cross?*

He couldn't see her face, but there was something in the sole of her bare foot tucked under her hip, in the tilt of her head, in the way her long, black hair fanned out against her back that Harvey found beautiful.

He wanted badly to say something, but he was never good at that. Never knew what to say. So he walked on, made it to the CVS, bought some ointment and gauze and then dressed his wound. On his way back from the store, his heart sped up as he saw that the girl was still there.

From this angle, he could see her face. Her full lips were set in a slight pout, as if she were unsatisfied with her work. Her brow was furrowed in concentration. She didn't notice him.

"Ahh," he whispered with a nod, able to see the image clearer than before. The birds looked like lollipops. Or maybe they were like popsicles. Frozen on sticks. *Bird pops. Very odd.* But they looked good, he had to admit.

She must have sensed someone staring and looked up. He hadn't realized how close he'd inched.

She shrieked and tried to cover her work with her arm. In doing so, she knocked over her little water jar. It spilled across the piece she'd been painting, smearing and washing away the image.

"Oh no!" she cried, quickly trying to blot the water with her sleeve. That just made it worse. "Oh, Suzie."

He wasn't sure what to do. He fumbled an apology and then bent down to try to help.

"No, no. Please. Just stop…please leave it. It's okay. It's fine…I'm fine."

She was flustered. He was flustered. Her fingers were shaking, her cheeks flushed. She quickly covered the rest of her papers with her hand and then hastily stacked them up. She was near tears, he could tell, and he tried again to apologize. She hurried to put her supplies back in her bag.

"You don't have to go," he tried. "I'll go. Ah, hell, I didn't mean to…"

"It's okay," she said. "It was nothing. It wasn't your fault. I just… They were nothing anyway. Please. It's fine."

He didn't know what to say. He clenched his teeth and felt his temper rising. He wanted to hit something. He wanted a way to make it better. He threw up his hands like he was pleading with her, or maybe like he was giving up, releasing what little he had left to give. But she wasn't looking at him. He limped off, his thumb throbbing. He passed the playground and left the park, back to the world.

He pictured her eyes when she had looked up in surprise. They were almost purple, like indigo. She was beautiful. But who had she seen? A crippled, lonely old man, no doubt.

Suddenly, the things he could have said to her came to him. He could have just told her that he thought she was a really good painter. Simple. Sweet. He could have said how much he liked those little frozen birds she was painting, that they weren't nothing. Not at all! He could have said that sometimes he feels like a frozen bird, too. How everyone has probably felt like a frozen bird at some point. Or, maybe, he even could have said that she had pretty eyes. Like the sea just before sunrise.

Instead, Harvey stood at the corner of the park nursing his thumb and waiting for the light to change. A woman crossed the other way, walking a groomed little poodle that was wearing a sweater. Harvey had the urge to kick it. To punt the crude-looking animal up over the power lines and out into the water.

The light changed. He stepped off the curb and was almost hit by some idiot making an illegal right on red. He flipped him off and then put his hands in his pockets. The fingers of his uninjured hand curled around a piece of carved wood.

Of course, he thought, *the bird!* He turned around quickly and then hustled, as best as he could, back toward the park gate, taking the half-finished hummingbird out of his pocket.

He would just show it to her. Or maybe he could give it to her. Yes, that's all he needed to do. A peace offering. He didn't have to say a thing. He could just hold it out to her. She would see it, and she would know. She would look at the bird, and then she would look at his face, and she would understand. She would see the real Harvey, who he'd been when he was younger, before the accident, before he came to the city. She would see it, and then she would understand.

Harvey walked back into the park, back past the playground, back toward the eucalyptus tree.

A few people were playing Frisbee. One couple walked arm and arm with a big lab. Some guy in a fur cap walked by mumbling to himself. But the girl was gone.

He looked up and down. The spot where her blanket had been just a couple minutes earlier was now just matted-down grass. No sign of her. Maybe he had the wrong tree? He looked everywhere. No. That was definitely the right tree.

Standing there in the middle of that park, Harvey wanted to yell something. God, what he wouldn't have done then to be able to step into the ocean and let the tide just carry him away.

He took the little bird out of his pocket. *Fucking thing*, he thought. *She wouldn't have liked it anyway*. He tried to break it, but he couldn't. He couldn't get a good hold on the stupid piece of dead wood. The bird was too small, too hard. His thumb was too sore.

He wanted to chuck it out of the park. But he didn't have the energy. He just tossed it aside, instead, like a spent cigarette butt. The bird didn't make a sound when it hit the ground. Harvey looked at the little, unfinished thing for a minute, half-submerged, sinking into the green. Then he hobbled away.

PART II.

A Dinner for Strangers

IT WAS JUST BEFORE the Earth began to shake. Eliza was sitting at the circulation desk of Plainview's central library. She pulled out her makeup mirror and looked at herself. Her face was covered in pale foundation. Her lips were bright red. Heavy mascara contrasted her pale-green eyes. She tilted the mirror down. A long, medieval-looking frock showed a good deal of her cleavage. Her fingernails were painted black. She tilted the mirror back up. There it was. In her otherwise jet-black hair, the damn silver streak.

Eliza first noticed the strands of gray about a year earlier. She stepped out of the shower one morning, wrapped herself in a towel, and wiped the glass. She plugged in the blow dryer, flipped the switch, and leaned in to look at herself through the steam.

"No way. No fucking way."

Wiping the glass again, Eliza cursed again. She wiped the glass a third time. She cursed a third time. Sure, she'd noticed a few gray hairs before, but nothing like this. Suddenly there was a whole shock of it just to the left of her part. She hollered for her mom.

Her mother came. "Oh, honey," she said, hugging her daughter. "It's not like it's such a big surprise." Eliza looked up at her mom's wave of gray in exactly the same place. Eliza's grandmother had the streak as well.

"Yeah, I know, but I'm way younger than you!"

Her mother scowled at her. "It happened to me about your age, too. It'll be okay."

"They're wiry," Eliza whined. "Almost curly. Were yours like this? I'm turning into an old fucking clown."

"Eliza. Stop it. It's not that bad."

"Of course *you're* going to say that. But it *is* that bad. It's really bad! I'm only twenty-six. I still live with my parents! What am I going to do now?"

Her mother made a half-hearted attempt to console her. "You've had your hair a different color nearly every season, honey. What's the difference between blue or pink and gray?"

"You really asking that? Big difference. *Huge* difference."

Eliza began plucking out the hairs with her fingers. She winced as she yanked out a whole clump.

"Stop that," her mother said. "I can't watch this." She turned and left the bathroom.

Eliza had been doing this whenever she spotted one. Mostly she just picked through with her thumb and forefinger. Sometimes she used tweezers. Up until that morning, she stayed more or less on top of them. But suddenly, there were many more than she could cull, more even than she could count.

Eliza became obsessed with getting out the hairs. Wherever she went, she brought her makeup mirror and pulled every silver strand she could. When she got up from her seat on the bus or the train, she left behind a layer of grays, a wispy covering that would blow away when the door opened.

When she walked, concerned only with those hairs, she bumped into people and signs. She walked smack into a tree. She was almost hit by a truck.

At some point in the summer, Eliza gave up. "I have to stop this," she told her mother. "I'm going to go bald."

"Or break your nose."

"And they're still there! I don't understand it. Where do they all come from?"

Her mother told her she should embrace it. "Or dye it?" she said.

"You didn't dye yours."

Eliza's mother had embraced her change by wearing more turtlenecks and sweaters, high-waisted jeans. She married the boy she'd been dating since high school. She started cooking casseroles. She basically entered middle age.

But Eliza wasn't willing to do that. Instead, she assumed a persona that fit her hair. She went out and bought a new wardrobe and makeup. Foundation called Manic Panic "Anemic," "Russian Red" lipstick, and the blackest eye shadow and liner she could find. She picked up a few satiny robes at the nearby vintage store, clothes that seemed suited for the bedroom or maybe for Halloween. She read books about witchcraft and the darker arts.

Once again, Eliza had recreated herself. Those around her had to go along. The more she got into the part, the more she came to like the streak. The more she liked the streak, the more she got into the part. For a time, she even considered bleaching her whole head.

Eliza's teen years had been a parade of different looks. She went from preppy to punk. She was straight-edge for a year. She was butch for a while. She was a hippie for a season.

This incarnation was different, though. Eliza was older, well out of college. Her parents had long assumed she'd gotten over what they called her "dress-up phases." Eliza knew her folks tried their best to be supportive. But they lived in the suburbs. The neighbors talked behind their backs. They looked at her funny. Eliza could tell. When her parents fought, it was often about her. When her dad chose not to join them for dinner at a restaurant, Eliza knew why.

It was time for her to leave home. Like most kids from the suburbs, Eliza decided to move to Plainview. "Go put that Literature degree we paid so much for to work," her father said. Surely, she could do better than the coffee shop she had been working at.

Eliza finally had the push she needed. And if she were going to move, then she could also work on the novel she always dreamed of writing. She would be like a Gothic, urban Virginia Wolf. She couldn't wait.

So BEGAN THE PROCESS of breaking ties that should have been long broken. The childhood bedroom. The home-cooked meals. The high school boyfriend.

Within a few months of deciding it was time to go, Eliza was sharing an outdated two-bedroom with a woman and her cat. The place had an old gas stove that she lit with a match. Eliza had a stack of blank composition books and a pencil case of ballpoints. Her closet was full of silky gowns and lacy bustiers.

Eliza hardly saw her roommate. The woman worked nights and slept late. Her cat, on the other hand, was always around. A black Persian, which took quickly to Eliza.

Plainview was a welcome relief at first. People didn't stare. People didn't talk about her behind her back. Soon Eliza forgot she was in character. It just became who she was. She didn't break out of it ever, even at home with the shades drawn.

"It's like, I don't know, like I've come out of hiding or something," she told her mom on the phone not long after moving. "No offense, but I had to get out of there." Her mom didn't say anything. "I'm not the weirdest one on the street anymore, Mom. Not by a long shot!"

But the honeymoon was short-lived. Although there were a lot more people in Plainview than her hometown, Eliza felt more alone than before. She cooked meals by herself. She went to yoga classes at the YMCA by herself. She tried to write by herself. She didn't make any real friends. Her ex stopped taking her calls. Eliza only had that cat. And even the cat, Eliza knew, just liked her because she fed her.

Eliza couldn't handle the weather. Cold and clammy. Every day started out the same shade of gray. "Like my hair," she told her mom. "So you think it's going to rain. I could get into that. You get an umbrella. Maybe you make some tea. You wear a sweater. But it never rains! By, like, eleven, the skies clear. It even gets hot. Then you have this sweater you're carrying around the rest of the day."

"That doesn't sound that bad," her mom offered.

"Yes. It *is* that bad! It's annoying. It's misleading. It's depressing."

Eliza had a hard time finding work. The obvious places weren't hiring: the gaming store, the party store, the tattoo parlors, the novelty shops.

Eventually, Eliza found work at the local library. The director said he liked the idea of having someone work the circulation desk who looked like a fictional character. He claimed not to be worried that she might scare off the children or be a distraction to those doing serious work. Eliza decided later that he just found her sexy.

"It's like having Catherine from *Wuthering Heights* right here in the library," he said. "Good for business."

Eliza thought the reference wasn't quite right, but she took the job. In addition to working the desk, Eliza helped with the weekly story time in the library's little story nook. The children loved her. A handful of parents complained that the lady reading to their kids looked somewhat like the bride of Frankenstein, but Eliza's light eyes were kind, and she told the children that she was "a good witch."

The regulars got used to her as well. Most of them didn't flirt with her. The director was the worst, actually. Eliza often caught him peering at her through spaces between the books on the shelves or taking odd routes through the library so he could pass just in front of or close behind her.

The work was hardly work. Mindless. Easy. It gave her plenty of time to write, which had been her hope when she took the job. The computer mounted beside her at the circulation desk only went to book-related sites, so she had little to distract her. Most of the day, Eliza wrote character sketches of the people who came into the library. Snapshots of loneliness.

❖

ELIZA WROTE ABOUT THE guy she dubbed Electronics Man. He didn't have a library card, so she didn't know his real name. The guy came in nearly every day, dressed in a frayed suit. He carried a briefcase full of papers and wore a backpack crammed with office equipment from the eighties and nineties: a huge calculator, two pairs of headphones, a bunch of mismatched power supplies, an old Toshiba laptop.

He laid them all out on a long table in the reading room, setting up his "desk" in the exact same order and arrangement each day. He never turned anything on, of course. Eliza doubted that any of the devices still worked.

He began by wiping down each piece with a pocket square. Then, after everything was ready and in place, he spent hours focused on his imaginary work. When the announcement came at 5:15 every day that the library would soon be closing, Electronics Man would look at his bare wrist, throw his hands up and mumble something about there never being enough time. Then he'd pack up his things and rush off.

Eliza decided he had been a middle manager of a large company. She pictured the office building in which he worked, imagined what his division was responsible for, described the framed photographs on his desk. Then came the layoffs. He hadn't seen them coming. When the boss called him into his office to fire him, Electronics Man had thought he was about to get promoted. He already picked a gift out in his mind to give to his wife. Losing his job was devastating. He'd been living paycheck to paycheck and owed a lot on his house and car. More than the financial blow, though, he was terribly ashamed. He never fully recovered. He didn't tell anyone, not his friends, not even his family. So he was in the library pretending he was still employed. He borrowed more and more money to keep up the charade, and now even debt collectors were after him.

Eliza came to believe the fiction she created. She greeted him with a big smile every time he came in, showing him great respect and empathy, misplaced though it may have been.

She also wrote about Russell. Everyone knew Russell. The guy with the canines. He actually lived on her block. She often saw him through her window coming back home from wherever he went in the morning. Russell had a library card, and he used it. All the time.

Sometimes he came several times a day, checking out old VHS tapes, obscure biographies, books on the Mayans. He was often going on about some new conspiracy theory. Russell was the only person who put suggestions in the suggestion box. He had a new notion each time he came in: a title they ought to add or a more sensible system for cataloguing the collection. Once he asked them to clean the microfiche projector, a piece of equipment only he used. Once he suggested they start selling Tab in the soda machine. Eliza wasn't sure if Tab was even still in production. Once he drew a map describing a different way to organize the stacks. The project would have required the library to be closed for months.

Eliza stitched together a story for Russell as well, using his random mutterings and her own imagination. Freshly married and just out of medical school, he had enlisted in Vietnam. Saw some terrible things, but he returned intact. He completed his residency, and all was good until the PTSD kicked in. Suddenly he'd scream or hit the ground and cover his head. The episodes started happening while he was seeing patients. He was often hearing the sound of approaching helicopters. The sound would intensify until he couldn't bear it. It happened once while he was operating. He tried to fight the hallucination, but it got so bad that he flinched and nearly killed the woman he was working on. He lost his medical license. That was the beginning of the slide.

Eliza felt terrible for Russell, too. She wanted to tell him that she understood, that it wasn't his fault.

Then there was the bird lady. Eliza thought she looked like a Maureen. Each time Maureen came in, she had a green parakeet sitting on her shoulder. The bird could talk. Eliza pictured fifty birds living with Maureen in her house. Most weren't in cages. She had names for each one of them and put feed right on the dining room table so they could eat beside her.

The first day Maureen brought the bird into the library, people made a fuss. The director had to be called. He approached her cautiously and tried to explain the no-pet policy.

"Really, it's nothing against birds," he told her. "No animals are allowed on the premises, unless they are assist animals."

Eliza overheard as Maureen tried to argue that her parakeet was a kind of assist animal, that it kept her blood pressure down. The director didn't relent. Eliza thought he handled it well and told him so. But apparently Maureen didn't think he had handled it well. She and the bird marched out in a huff. And when Maureen returned the very next day, the very same bird was on her shoulder. Once again, the director tried to talk to her. Eliza couldn't make out what they were saying, but it seemed everyone, even the bird, was yelling. Eliza was sure Maureen and the bird would be thrown out for good. But Maureen didn't leave. After the yelling subsided, she switched the bird over to her other shoulder, strode indignantly to a table beside the newspaper rack and sat down.

Trying to salvage his pride, the director walked over to Eliza's desk and explained that the bird would temporarily be allowed to stay. He restated Maureen's arguments that the old protocol discriminated against pets and pet owners. He seemed suddenly convinced the bird wouldn't cause any disruptions. "In fact," he went on, pointing toward a few of the people sitting at the tables, "that bird will probably behave better than most of the rest of them."

Eliza raised her eyebrows but didn't respond.

"So for now, Eliza, the bird stays."

Eliza thought about these people all the time. They stayed with her when she left work. At the gym, on her walks home, or while she ate dinner. Where did they go when the library closed? Did they have homes? Did they have families? Did they see each other outside the library? What would they say if they did?

Eliza had always ignored the crazies, the homeless, the lost and lonely. It seemed everyone in Plainview, as liberal as they may have been, averted their eyes. But Eliza couldn't avoid them anymore.

She began wondering about God. Eliza wasn't raised religiously, but in private she prayed. And more and more, she prayed for these people who came into the library.

"Forget about our book-lending part," she told the director one afternoon. "We need this place because it gives them somewhere to go."

The director didn't say anything at first. He was trying to see down Eliza's top.

"Seriously," she said, leaning back and pulling up her chemise. "They'd be lost without us here."

"What's that?"

"I said they'd be lost without this place."

He nodded but didn't say anything.

"You're not listening to me."

"Yes, I am. Of course, I am."

"Look, they're waiting outside when we unlock the doors. Some have big backpacks. Some are talking to themselves. Who knows how long they wait for us to open up."

He blinked into focus and started to listen. "Your point?"

"*My point*? Don't you think it makes what we do important?"

He didn't answer immediately. Eliza asked again.

"Eliza, the library isn't a shelter. That's not why we're here. That's not why I'm here, at least. I have a degree in information science. I'm not a social worker."

Eliza looked up at him in confusion. She thought about the services their library offered: job training, family counseling, ESL classes. She started to argue and then gave up.

"I'm not a social worker," he repeated. "That's not why libraries exist. We're a research institution."

Eliza left in frustration when her shift ended. She called home and tried to talk to her parents about it. Her mother wasn't interested, either. And when there was a lull in Eliza's monologue, her mother said, "Honey, your father and I were wondering…"

Eliza knew immediately where it was going.

"Are you still dressing in those…I mean, are you still?"

Eliza didn't say anything. She wanted her mother to have to come out and say it.

"Are you still in your Elvira phase?"

"My *Elvira phase*?"

"You know what I mean…"

Eliza was silent.

"Oh, honey. We just thought that maybe…"

"Jesus. Look, it's not a phase. Get over it. And that's not why I called." Why she had called was fading.

"Well, we just hoped," her mom continued.

"I know what you hoped. I don't care what you hoped."

"Don't talk to me like that!"

"You're always hoping I'll be someone else."

"Stop it, Eliza. That's not true. You know that's not true. We've always supported you. We just want what's best—"

Eliza cut her off. "Mom, this is who I am. Get used to it."

"But it's not who you are. It's not who you were."

"You never knew who I was."

There was a long silence. Eliza almost apologized. But then it was her dad on the line.

"Listen, sweetheart, you know your mom and I love you. You're so beautiful, sweetheart. We just want you to be yourself. You don't have to try to be someone you're not."

She had heard this so many times from them. It inevitably made her want to shock them more, to dress more radically, bring stranger boys home, stay out even later. This time, though, Eliza didn't argue. She was too tired to argue. She let him finish, asked if he was done, and then she hung up on him.

Eliza began sulking at the circulation desk, began finding it harder and harder to write. She would sit there, staring at her makeup mirror or blankly at the door.

Sometimes a patron would have to ask several times before Eliza understood the question.

And soon, without knowing it, she was at her hair again, trying to separate the grays from the blacks, trying to pluck them out of her scalp.

THE DAY OF THE earthquake, Eliza was at her desk looking at her little mirror and messing with her hair.

"Something bothering you, Miss?"

It was Adam, the kid who came in after school to shelve books. Eliza didn't hear him. He asked again.

"Well, doesn't it bug you?"

"Doesn't what bug me, Miss Martin?"

She nodded toward a few of the people in the room. "Them," she said in the librarian's whisper-yell she'd perfected working there. "All of them. How lonely they are? How hopeless?"

"Uh, I don't know. I guess, Miss Martin."

"Don't *Miss Martin* me. I'm not that much older than you, Adam."

That wasn't true. They both knew it.

"Sorry Miss...I mean...Eliza. What are you talking about?"

"I'm talking about the fact that they're crazy. These people are totally crazy. They have nowhere to go. A lot of them don't. They're loners. Doesn't it get to you? Being around them all the time? Doesn't it depress you?"

He was probably sixteen. He definitely wasn't thinking about them. He shrugged.

"Is this what life is?" she challenged him.

"Are you asking me?"

"You don't think about it at all, do you?"

"Not really."

"Must be nice."

"At least they have this place, I guess."

"Okay! Exactly," she said too loudly. People turned and looked, so she started whispering again. "That's what I've realized lately. This is it. This is their home. That's what we're here for. This is what this place is all about."

It was right then that all hell broke loose. Eliza noticed it first as a strange buzzing, like static electricity or a Geiger counter. Maybe it was the power lines out front. When she tried to recollect it, it was definitely something electric she noticed first. She was talking to Adam about the people in the library when the strange crackling and popping began.

Then it felt like a truck might have crashed into the building. She felt the impact, and there was terrible noise. Eliza would describe it like a thunder she felt in her gut that wouldn't stop.

Then it seemed the Earth turned liquid. The shelves of children's books rose several feet and then thundered down. The lights went out.

Eliza rose from her chair but quickly lost her balance. She fell to the floor. It was too late to get safely to a doorway or wherever it was people were supposed to go.

Books were everywhere, flying left to right, right to left, even up, it seemed. Plaster rained down from the ceiling. The white dust covered Eliza's hair. In different circumstances, she might have made an ironic remark about her hair. But not then. She crawled beneath a desk, covering herself as best she could with her arms.

The quake lasted a little more than a minute. Eliza felt like it would never stop. Cradling her head in her hands, Eliza closed her eyes. Things grew strangely quiet.

And then she was eight again. It must have been Christmas Eve, for Eliza was in the blue wool dress with silver trim that her mother made. The fire was lit, too, and as far as Eliza could remember her father only lit the fire on Christmas Eve. A Burl Ives record played, and her mother hummed along from the kitchen. Those wooden dolls from around the world were out on the mantle, and the fake gold bell with the string hung from the entryway ceiling. Eliza used to have to jump to pull that string.

Then her mom was helping her get into her mittens and huge coat. She was walking between her parents toward town. She could feel her father's leather-gloved hand holding hers. Candles in brown bags lined the sidewalks. Lights were strung across the streets. Wreaths hung on the lampposts.

They turned from Walnut onto Main. Eliza was watching her breath in the chilly air, trying to send it out in thin streams. Soon she could hear people and sense the excitement. There were long tables set right in the middle of the road. A big pot of mulled wine simmered over a couple Coleman camp stoves. The kids got hot cider. Women ladled bowls of some kind of stew or soup.

Loaves of bread were passed. It was the town's annual Christmas Eve dinner. Everyone was invited. And many came, more people than could sit at the tables. They stood around eating and shaking hands, wishing each other a Merry Christmas.

When the meal was over there was caroling, and then the families said goodbye and walked back to their houses. Eliza and her parents went to mass. It was the only time of the year they went to church. Still, Eliza felt so safe there. Safer there than maybe anywhere. The smell of incense and stone. She closed her eyes and talked to God, praying for her parents and her cousins, for her friends at school, for peace.

WHEN ELIZA OPENED HER eyes, the shaking was over, but the library was a wreck. People were running for the exit, yelling, pushing, and shoving. Russell had managed to leave as soon as the quake began, Eliza saw him speed walking out the door before she got under the table. He was mumbling about someone named Lucy. Eliza saw the director leave, too. He ran out, just behind Russell, pushing someone out of his way to get to the door. *That didn't seem right*, Eliza thought.

Eliza was the very last to leave. She crawled slowly out from under the table, as if under a spell. She brushed herself off. She helped people make their way to the door. She checked the bathrooms. She even started to flip some chairs, like the night janitor did before he swept.

As she stepped out onto the street, Eliza tried to pray. But she couldn't. She couldn't find God then. She didn't know where to look. Everything was a mess. The pavement was cracked. The sidewalk buckled. Trees were down. A car had crashed into a storefront. Alarms and sirens whaled. Eliza could hear someone crying. The sky was perfectly blue, but the streets looked like a terrible storm had torn through.

Many of the library regulars were clustered at the foot of the steps, spit out like there'd been a shipwreck. Eliza wondered what they were waiting for. A rescue boat?

Eliza saw people across the street and in front of the other buildings furiously trying to make calls and send texts, to check in, to make sure loved ones were okay. But no one in the huddle in front of Eliza was calling anyone.

"It was a big one," she heard someone say.

"At least a six," said another.

"Five-nine," Electronics Guy declared, and people near him nodded like he would know.

It was the first time she'd seen these people under anything other than the fluorescents. They looked even worse: paler, less normal, like one big, dysfunctional gang, some group from an assisted living center out on a field trip. And that made Eliza their leader. That made her responsible for them, like she should tell them to buddy up or count off. She felt they were waiting on her to tell them when it was safe to go back in, if it would ever be safe to go back in. And, if not, where they should go.

A fireman came by and asked if everyone was okay. Then he told the crowd to disperse. A couple people left, but most of them remained, just staring up at her. Eliza didn't know what to tell them. She wanted so badly to have something positive to say, but what was there? Finally, she turned and left. The look on her face said

I'm sorry. But there was nothing to be done. She turned back to look before rounding the corner. Many were still standing there.

AND THEN AN AFTERSHOCK came. Eliza was in the park, a pretty good place to be, she figured. Still, she didn't know about aftershocks, and so it scared her even more than the initial earthquake, made her almost nauseous, the way the Earth moved, the way the grass rolled.

Eliza sat on the ground, held her knees. And then she did pray. She prayed for her parents, like she used to. And she prayed for herself. That she could find what she was meant to do, who she was meant to be. She prayed for the people back in front of the library, for Electronics Man and Maureen. She prayed for Russell.

As she stood up to start again for home, Eliza had an idea. She would throw the Christmas Eve dinner right there in Plainview. Christmas wasn't even that far off. Just like the one in her town growing up. She could make invitations. She could pass them out in the library, if it reopened by then. Otherwise, she could go looking on the street for the people to invite. She could slip some under the doors in her apartment building. Put them in the neighbors' mailboxes. People might bring a dish if they wanted to. Or they didn't have to bring anything at all. They could just come.

Eliza thought about all the characters she'd met since moving, all the people who probably had no one else to eat with on Christmas Eve. She even began imagining a seating arrangement. The professor who lost his mind should meet Russell. The man who was reading all those books about bridges might like to meet that Ahab-looking guy with the limp. Maureen and her bird might talk to the lady who makes all those junk sculptures. Maybe the girl with the bangs and the cool tattoo would want to talk to the woman with all the trinkets in her window. The woman who paints those watercolor popsicle birds, well, Eliza wanted to sit beside her.

Yes, a public pot luck. Christmas Eve. It was a perfect plan. A perfect way to recover. It would give them a place to go, something to look forward to. It would give her something to look forward to.

Eliza made it back to her place. She wasn't sure what she was going to find. There was a lot of damage. A pipe had burst, and there was water leaking from the ceiling. The cabinet doors had flung open and most of the dishes were shattered on the floor. The glass in her bedroom window was gone. Her dresser had toppled over. The cat was hiding in the closet. He had peed all over her shoes.

When Eliza went to the bathroom, she noticed that the mirror had cracked. Only a few shards remained. She peered into a sliver to look at herself. With all the plaster still in her hair, Eliza couldn't tell the gray from the black. For the first time in a long time, she didn't care. She brushed as much of the dust out as possible and then took out her phone, relieved that it still had charge and, miraculously, full bars.

Her mother cried at the sound of her voice. Eliza almost did, too.

"It's okay, Mom. It's okay. I'm fine."

TEA FOR TWO

"WHAT IN GOD'S NAME was I thinking, Henry?" Rose whispered. She set her teacup on the box that doubled as her chair. "Feels like I'm barely floating, lately. Like I'm on some kind of cardboard boat."

Boxes filled the basement. She couldn't even see the far wall. "Hard to handle this all on my own, dear."

Forty years had passed since the last time Rose had moved. The kids weren't even born yet, of course. Christ, she was only twenty-seven at the time. Henry, fresh back from Vietnam, was only thirty-five. She could still picture the day he returned from the bank in his crisp khakis with the news that they could finally afford to buy a real home.

Rose had done most of the packing that time, too. It was she who wrapped her mother-in-law's porcelain tea set, including the cup she'd just set down, and the silver salt and pepper shakers. It was she who had cleaned out the drawers and ironed and folded the linen before boxing it all up. It was he who constantly had tried to distract her from her tasks, humming sappy love songs, slipping his arm around her waist and twirling her around the linoleum kitchen floor. Henry was a terrible singer. He wasn't the greatest dancer either, come to think of it. But how she had loved when he took her in his arms.

She knew, of course, it couldn't have been all good. But as Rose remembered, making that new house their home was a glowing time, like when they'd picked out that shade of cream together and painted the living room. "Old World Romance" was the color they chose. They laughed about the name, but that was really what the color was called. At one point she rolled that roller, thick with paint, right over Henry's hand and shirtsleeve. He didn't even get angry. He did dab paint on both her cheeks, but he wasn't angry. Rose couldn't remember a single time he'd raised his voice against her. In all those years, not a single time.

"You used to tell me I was beautiful every day," Rose said to him. "Remember how you used to say that when you were at my side, you could walk into a room naked and no one would even notice you?" Rose blushed at the thought. "That was such a sweet thing to say."

She sipped her cooling tea and set it back on the box. "They don't make men like you anymore. Wendy certainly didn't find one." Rose smoothed her slacks and re-crossed her legs. As she did, she knocked over the teacup. It rolled off the box and shattered on the floor.

"Oh, Rose!" She stood and went to get some paper towel and the broom. "I'm sorry, Henry."

Henry had been dead for more than two decades, even longer than they'd been married. Their kids were both grown, with kids of their own. The floorboards in their house, once unscratched and shining, were scuffed and well-worn. Those living room walls they'd painted together had long ago been repainted by professionals. Still, they were peeling again.

Rose's granddaughter was actually the first to suggest that she sell the house and move out of the suburbs. "You should move to the city, Grandma. It's *soooo* awesome there."

That was how she put it. As if it would be as easy for Rose to move to Plainview as it was for her granddaughter to send a text. The child proceeded to list everything that was just *so awesome* about it there. Even listening to the list was exhausting. Rose had to cut her off.

"Don't be silly, dear. People my age move out of cities not into them."

"You could get a roommate! We can find you a place on Craigslist! Look here, Grandma. I have the app."

"I don't even know what an app is," Rose smiled, pushing the phone aside.

Much to her family's surprise, however, Rose actually began to come around. Not the roommate or the Craigslist parts, of course, but the city part.

Nothing was keeping her in that house, she told Phillip on the phone. "I can't be here anymore. Not sure what changed, Phillip. But I keep feeling like I've lost something when I'm here. Like all of you should still be here. When you're not, it doesn't feel right."

Phillip said he understood. Still, he pushed for her to move somewhere more sensible. "Palm Desert, maybe?"

Rose laughed. "I'm not going to just sit around, get tan, and die, dear." She wanted to go into the world, not run from it.

He was silent for a while. She thought maybe they had been disconnected. "Well, you could always come live with us," he finally offered.

"Don't be silly. No one would want that."

"I just worry about you all alone, Mom."

"Alone? I'm alone here. In Plainview, there will be people everywhere. Please. *Don't be alone.* That's exactly why I need to do this, Phillip."

❖

WHEN ROSE PLAYED BRIDGE with her group, nearly all they talked about was the plan. Barbara told her how brave she was. Clara repeated the sentiment. Gail kept saying that she didn't think she would ever have enough courage to move. On and on they went, almost making Rose wonder if she were, in fact, brave enough, if she weren't fooling herself.

Still, she kept up a strong front. "Please, don't be ridiculous," she would tell them. "Yes, you could. You all could. We aren't children, you know. We may not be young," she smiled, "but we're not helpless either."

"What about getting mugged?" Barbara asked.

"Or lost?" Clara said.

"You heard about that news story a few years ago where some guy mugged the hundred-and-one-year-old lady, right?" Barbara asked. "A hundred and one years old!"

"Oh, stop it," Rose said sharply. "That was a crazy story. Besides, that was New York. This is Plainview. It's totally different."

Still, that night Rose couldn't sleep. "Is it all that different, Henry? Am I crazy?"

❖

DESPITE HER GROWING ANXIETY, Rose met with a realtor. They found a small one bedroom a few blocks from the library and the park. The rent was more than Rose thought the place worth, but if she got what they said she might for the old house, then she calculated she could live modestly until…well, for long enough.

Of course, that meant that she couldn't bring most of her old things. The new place was quite a downgrade, not even a quarter the size of her home. So Rose spent hours in her musty, old basement trying to figure out what to do with a lifetime of stuff. Boxes of photo albums and strips of negatives, boxes of yearbooks, boxes of postcards and letters she and Henry had sent each other, boxes of art projects, of baseball cards, of electric trains and toy soldiers. One box, apparently full of magazines, was labeled *TIME*. Another said *Tiki Mugs*. "Did we even own tiki mugs?" she asked.

Two big wardrobe boxes were full of winter clothes. "One season, but two huge boxes?" Rose shook her head, thinking about a box stuffed with all the parkas and mittens they used to stuff their kids into.

All those moments and memories had been squished into cardboard and taped shut. Boxed. Packed up. Sealed. Filed away for some other time that never came. "Maybe I should have just thrown them all away?"

Rose didn't like looking at her life that way. "It's like canopic jars, Henry. Each part of me, of us, is in a separate box now."

Rose was taping colored tags on the tops of the boxes. She stopped to wipe her brow with a handkerchief. "Everything down here was so precious back then. It would have been unthinkable to throw it away. That's why we kept it all. But most of this stuff has been sealed for so long. Like it's from someone else's life. Tell me, how precious could it have been?" Rose walked up the basement stairs and turned off the light. "I wish you could answer me."

Rose invited her kids to visit and put Post-its on anything they wanted. Wendy and her son didn't even come. Phillip and his daughters came. But they only wanted a few silly things: the scalloped dish that held the candied nuts she always laid out during the holidays, a set of glasses with Norman Rockwell scenes on them, a couple of candlesticks, the 1978 *Encyclopedia Britannica*. Nothing that Rose really cared about, though. Nothing significant.

"What about Phillip's first baseball mitt, Henry? Or the dining room table we ate all our meals on? What about the old Polaroid? Who cares that it doesn't take pictures anymore? And the rocking chair where I nursed them. What about that?"

Rose tried to breath. She felt she was on the verge of a panic attack. "Everything you worked so hard to afford, Henry… Everything we lived in and on and with. Why don't they want any of it?"

Two small boxes said *Wendy's Room*. Rose ran her hand across the dusty top of one.

Oh, Rose, she said to herself, *not now.* She felt the tears coming and crumpled down onto one of the boxes.

Wendy was their firstborn, her baby. She had always been the fragile one. And maybe that was at the root of it all. Rose had been too concerned, always too afraid that

Wendy would get bruised by the world. Too afraid to let her make her own mistakes. "Of course that was going to make her rebel. You always warned me. But you were the one who knew how to talk to her."

When they fought, Wendy yelled at Rose for not approving of anything she did—what she ate, how short her skirts were, why she insisted on smoking in her bedroom. Rose yelled at Wendy for being disrespectful, not thinking enough about her future, making one bad decision after another.

Shortly after Henry died, Wendy came home to announce she was engaged. Rose didn't say the right thing. She had never approved of anyone Wendy had dated, but she certainly didn't like this one. So it all came out. Flooding out. Years of pent-up feelings.

Rose didn't receive the wedding invitation until ten days before the ceremony, making her assume Wendy didn't really want her there at all. The marriage only lasted a year, and Rose was unable to hold back the "I told you so." That pushed them even further apart.

❖

THE DOORBELL RANG. ROSE lurched back into the present. "Coming," she yelled, rising and crossing the sea of cardboard. It was the movers.

"You're early," she said, leading them into the house. "I was told that never happened with movers."

The head guy didn't crack a smile. He took off his cap and eyed his clipboard. There were three of them and a twenty-six footer parked in the driveway. Rose led him into the basement.

"Just the pieces and boxes marked with red tags."

The team leader's eyebrows rose. He must not have read the whole job memo. There was hardly anything marked with red tags. Rose explained that Goodwill would be coming the next morning for some of the boxes, and that the rest was going to the dump.

"Forgive me, Henry," she said as she turned from the movers. "I did my best."

❖

ROSE'S NEW APARTMENT WAS on the fourth floor of a drab building with a dimly-lit elevator and old, brown carpeting in the hallways. The landlord had gone on and on about the fancy new appliances, none of which impressed Rose. His eyes kept drifting down her body, something Rose hadn't noticed in a long time. She did not appreciate it.

That landlord had also boasted about the "great walk score" the place had, whatever that meant. He said that if Rose figured out the bus system, she could get almost anywhere.

So that's what she told everyone who called.

"Oh it's just great," she'd say without hesitation. "Did you know the walk score is an eighty-eight?"

Gail and Barbara were impressed.

"And with the buses, well, I don't even need a car," she told them. "I can get anywhere!"

Phillip called twice a week in the beginning.

"Well, what do you do all day, Mom?"

"What do I do?"

"Yeah, how do you get around?"

"How do I get around? I walk is how…or I take the bus."

"But where do you go? What do you do?"

"Where do I go? Oh, all over the place. The movies. I go to restaurants. I walk through the park. I watch the people. I do all sorts of things. Don't worry, Phillip. I'm fine. I love it here."

The truth, though, was that Rose didn't love it, and she wasn't exactly okay. She double-locked the front door immediately when she got home. Loud cars cruised by the building all night, the bass from their stereos rattling her windows. The buses screeched. The neighbors fought.

Rose didn't feel safe walking. She had only tried to take the bus once, and that had not gone well. She got on going the wrong direction and ended up in a part of town she'd never seen before and hoped never to see again.

"Henry, please," she whispered when the driver let her out. "Please take me home."

Eventually, Rose found someone who helped her find a taxi. It was a sixty-five-dollar mistake. And when she finally made it back to her apartment, she dropped her purse by the door, her hand aching from clutching it so tightly. She collapsed onto her couch.

Rose awoke disoriented. It was the middle of the night. She reached around until she finally found the lamp and turned it on. She slowly scanned the apartment. It could have been anyone's. The walls were mostly bare. A picture of Henry and a few pictures of the grandchildren were on a shelf, but that was all.

She had to go to the bathroom and got up carefully from the couch. She walked across the room, opened a door, and stepped straight into the coats hanging in the closet. Scared the hell out of her. Rose barely made it to the bathroom in time. It was all she could do not to fall apart.

Eventually, she went into the kitchen and found the light. Her cupboards were mostly empty. A package of saltines, two tins of tuna, some packets of Lipton Noodle Soup, a box of Earl Grey. She had brought her old tea set with its three remaining cups. Since moving, Rose had only used one of them. She took one down then and put the water on.

A precut cantaloupe in a plastic shell was starting to rot in her refrigerator. She threw it out. There was a tub of margarine. A pint of cottage cheese. Two little fat-free yogurt cups. And that idiotic pullout freezer drawer below? Well, apart from an untouched pint of Häagen-Dazs vanilla, that, too, was empty.

"Ever feel like you're some place longer than you're meant to be, Henry?" The teapot whistled. She let it whistle. "Like maybe you're at a fair and a storm comes, so everyone leaves, but for some reason you're still there. Do you know what I mean?"

❖

OVER THE LIP OF her teacup, Rose noticed fingerprints on the refrigerator. She put her cup down and went to wipe them off. There was dried lettuce stuck under the edge of the counter. She cleaned that, too. She began seeing crumbs and dirt and dust everywhere. The floors. The walls. Smudges and streaks. The more Rose looked, the more she saw. The windows were grimy. The entryway needed to be mopped. The door handles needed polishing. There were cobwebs in corners. The oven was caked with grease. *I've only used the oven twice! How could it be so filthy?*

Rose started cleaning. As the sky lightened, she was still cleaning. She became obsessed with keeping the place clean. Dusting. Spraying. Scrubbing. The window frames, the sills, the mantel. The baseboards. The cupboards. The tops of the shelves. The bottoms of shelves. She picked up and shook out the rug in the entryway. She pushed around furniture. She made and remade the bed. She rearranged the pillows on the couch. Every day, and sometimes twice. If she were honest with herself, if she really was going to tell Phillip what she did with her days, it was this. She went through cleaning supplies the way her family used to go through cartons of milk.

COMING BACK FROM THE store one day with more Windex and Brillo Pads, she rode the elevator with the young mother who lived down the hall. Rose saw her often with her little son. She had long, black hair like Wendy's, or at least like Wendy used to have.

Whenever Rose saw her coming or going, the younger woman smiled, but they had never talked. Her little boy had full cheeks and a messy mop of brown curls. Probably two or three, Rose guessed, about the same age as her granddaughter Emma. He liked to run up and down the halls, despite his mother's pleading and eventual yelling that he slow down and stay quiet. She must have been raising him alone. At least Rose had never noticed a father. She'd never seen any grandparents either.

In the elevator, Rose could tell she was upset. She felt like she should say something but didn't know what. She didn't want to pry. Rose had little confidence in her ability to talk to younger women.

They rode up together silently. Just as the doors were about to open, the girl dropped her keys.

"Oh, damn it," she cried.

Rose held the door open as the woman bent to pick them up. As she did, her tote bag tipped and several pieces of art paper spilled out. Rose saw a smudged out bird on one of them.

The woman hurriedly stuffed the papers back in her bag and collected her keys. "I'm sorry."

"Don't be silly," Rose smiled warmly. "Can I give you a hand?" Rose asked gently.

"No thank you," she said.

"Looks like it's been one of those days," Rose tried, laying a hand on her shoulder. The woman jumped at the touch.

"I guess it has." She took a breath as if she might speak, but she exhaled and shook her head. "It's okay. I'm fine."

The elevator door opened, and the young woman motioned for Rose to go out first.

Rose took a few steps and paused. "Well, I'm just down the hall, dear. Number four-oh-five. Right over there." She pointed a few doors down. "If you need anything. Anytime."

"Oh," the woman said. "Well, okay. Thank you."

Rose watched her walk off. The woman looked back and tried to smile. Rose added, "Henry and I raised two of our own, you know. I remember how it can be sometimes."

They went into their own apartments and closed their doors. Rose missed Wendy terribly then. She almost picked up the phone. "Can't you make her call, Henry?"

Rose thought about going back to knock on her neighbor's door. Maybe she could bring her some cookies or something. Yes, for her son. That would be a nice thing to do. So Rose went to the cupboard. But of course, there weren't any cookies in there. There wasn't anything in there. *How could I not have any cookies?* she thought, opening another cupboard that held her dishes. *I always used to have cookies.*

She went to the window and saw some children playing on the street. She noticed some streaks in the glass and started for the Windex. But when she caught a glimpse of her reflection, she paused. "What am I doing, Henry?" Her voice was shaking. She wanted to turn away from the glass, but she couldn't take her eyes off her reflection. She looked so old. She gripped the sill with both hands.

Rose wasn't sure how long she'd been standing there or how long the knocking had been going on, but at some point she realized a voice was calling her.

"Hello?"

She tried to straighten herself up.

"It's Suzie. From down the hall? From the elevator?"

"Oh yes, dear. I'm coming. Just a minute."

When the door opened, Suzie thought the older woman's eyes looked red. "Am I interrupting? I'm sorry if this is a bad time."

"Oh no, no. Not at all. Pease come in."

"Are you sure?"

"Yes. Please. Of course, I'm sure. I was actually…well, no, you are definitely not interrupting anything."

"It's just…" and then it was Suzie's turn to cry.

Rose instinctively reached out to hug her. Suzie let herself be held, and Rose felt so good finally having someone to hold.

"Come. Sit down," Rose said after a minute. She walked her to the couch. "My name is Rose."

"Thank you, Rose," Suzie said, sniffling. "I'm sorry. How embarrassing."

"Don't be sorry. You don't ever need to be sorry with me."

"You're kind. I can only stay a little bit. I have to get my son at daycare soon."

"Your boy is adorable."

Suzie smiled and reached for a tissue to blow her nose. "Your place is so clean."

"You think so? I don't …"

"Really," she laughed a stuffed-up laugh. "You should see my place."

Rose smiled. "I don't have much to offer you, but I can make you some tea. Do you drink tea?"

"I do, Rose. Thank you. I'd love some."

THE FREE BRONTOSAURUS

A BLUE POLKA-DOT RIBBON came first.

"I was just out here sweeping the steps," Martha told Carl, holding the little tattered strip of fabric up for him to see. She'd been out on the stoop, drinking coffee, waiting for him to get back from campus.

Carl looked confused.

"I know," Martha continued. "Not sure why I decided to sweep either. Almost *whooshed* the thing away." She laughed, tucked her hair behind her ear and smiled that impish smile, the same one he'd so fallen for when they first met. "Beauty, isn't it?" She ran a finger along the ribbon like it was a string of pearls.

Carl smiled awkwardly and slid his horn-rimmed glasses higher on the bridge of his nose. He'd worn that style frame since grade school. He squinted, unsure exactly what it was he was looking at.

"It's nice," he tried.

"I used to wear ones just like this when I was little. Look." And she began tying her honey-colored hair into pigtails. She only had the one ribbon though, so she was only able to tie up the left side. Carl laughed.

"You're laughing at me." She gave him a fake pout and pushed at his chest. "Don't laugh at me."

"No, no. I'm not. You look adorable, Marth. Really adorable…it's just…"

Carl pulled her toward him and kissed her forehead, and then he kissed her upper lip. He held her at arms length, looking at her sweetly. "I love you."

She smiled and pressed her mouth against his collarbone, her body into his. Soon they were at it again.

His fingertips found that hollow in the small of her back and followed it down. Her breath was heavy on his neck. They rushed up and into the house. He tugged off his tie and clumsily unbuttoned his shirt. She pulled her T-shirt up and over her head, pressing her small breasts against his chest. He worked a hand through her hair, then he traced a line with his nails down her backbone, all the way down her inner thigh. She undid his belt. Tore off his pants. Her hands were all over him. He rolled her lace underwear down her legs. She flung them aside with a bare foot.

It had been like this for a few months now. Carl wasn't sure what had changed, but he certainly wasn't complaining.

They made love like lions. Ravenously. Clawingly. Wildly.

When they collapsed onto the living room couch, their hearts still beating fast, Martha picked the ribbon up off the floor. She lay in Carl's arms, looking at a pattern of light on the wall. She twirled the ribbon around her finger, her violet eyes shining like river stones.

"I remember exactly how these felt in my hair when I was little. How they pulled when my mom did them up too tight. God, I never could sit still."

"Still can't," he smiled.

She pursed her lips. "I'm serious, Carl. How can I remember it so clearly? I still feel it. Ugh. I hated when she combed it. Like she was brushing a sheep or something. She'd squeeze me with her knees so tightly to hold me in place, you know, so she could tie the bows… Used to call it the *knee hug.* 'Here comes the knee hug,' she'd say. It hurt!"

The sun was sinking lower, the light beginning to illuminate the upper half of the living room wall.

"Look at that light," Carl said. "Like we're inside a glass of wine."

Martha smiled. They were quiet for a while, peaceful.

"Funny," she said softly.

"What is?"

"The things you come to miss."

Carl took the back of her hand to his mouth. He kissed it and held her palm against his cheek.

❖

THAT RIBBON CHANGED THE way Martha looked at the world. Over the next weeks and months, Martha found things all over the place. A piece of driftwood in the park that looked like remarkably like Abe Lincoln's face, top hat and all. Undeniable.

"God or man," she said to herself, "whoever made you, you're totally awesome." She brought him home. How could she not?

"Jesus, Marth," Carl said. "Where the hell did you find that?"

"By the lake! Right on that little trail around the back of it. Stopped me dead in my tracks. There were hikers going who didn't see it. Not me. 'That's our greatest president lying down there,' I said to myself."

Carl cracked up. She loved when he laughed at her jokes.

They made love like minks. Their bodies entwined, wrapped around each other, every part touching. Noses. Stomachs. Thighs. Feet.

A little porcelain elephant was next. One ear was broken, but it was otherwise intact.

"Someone must have left him," she explained, holding it up for Carl to see. "Sitting there on the bench at the bus stop. Little thing looked like he was just waiting for a bus!" Martha put it in the guest bedroom. Named him Eugene.

They made love like eagles. Locked together, they twirled. They soared. They fell. They soared again.

Martha found an old diving helmet. It was out on the curb in front of a seafood restaurant that was going out of business. The helmet was dented. The metal corroded. She thought Carl would love it. He did.

"Beautiful isn't it? In a tragic sort of way?"

"It sure is." he told her. "It sure is."

They made love like dolphins. Smoothly. Slowly. Tenderly.

Martha became obsessed with all things nautical. Lighthouses. A miniature wooden captain's wheel. A broken sextant. Many of these she found on walks down by the marina. In trash heaps. Behind buildings. Some were broken. Some just needed paint. She brought them all home. Several she touched up. Others she left as she found them. She put them all on display.

"You're on a real roll!" he told her.

When they went to the seashore, they gathered sea glass. Martha said the blue pieces looked like sapphires. Carl said they looked like her eyes. They collected driftwood. They found shells. Once she even brought home a large bucket of sand. She poured the whole pail carefully onto the sill. "To help with the display," she announced.

Carl was a little surprised by that move, but he nodded in tacit consent.

They made love like teenagers, recklessly, desperately. Against the shower tiles. Over the arm of the sofa. On the kitchen floor. Out on the back deck.

Meanwhile, their home was being transformed and starting to attract the neighbors' attention. Martha's discoveries were everywhere. On tables and shelves. Hanging from hooks. Even in the front yard. Nearly every flat space was taken up by some piece or another. Each had a story. Each became precious to her.

Carl wasn't sure what precipitated the change, but with all the sex, he didn't mind. Martha knew, though. She definitely knew. She had stopped taking the pill.

❖

YEARS AGO, NEW TO the city and not yet married, they both had said they never wanted to have children. But they'd been drinking then. They were flirting. Even at the time, Martha wasn't totally sure she meant it, but Carl seemed to, and so she went along with it. When Martha turned thirty, though, something in her body clearly changed.

She tried bringing it up a time or two, in subtle ways. She asked in joking tones, faking sarcasm. She might point out a particularly cute kid or a dad pushing his son on a swing. She was testing the waters, checking whether he was having any of the same thoughts.

He wasn't. He wasn't thinking about it at all. Carl taught physics at the university. He hadn't made tenure yet. He didn't have time for kids. His best friend in the department didn't have a kid. In fact, few of his colleagues had kids.

Martha was afraid to be blunt. Afraid he'd get angry, that it would become an issue. Instead, she just kept trying to find some little opening.

So her birth control pill went into the toilet each day instead of her mouth. It was the first time she'd kept something from him, or at least something this important.

She knew it was wrong, but Martha found ways to rationalize it. Carl would be a great dad. They would be great parents. Martha believed down deep he actually wanted a baby. *How could he not want a baby?*

She kept resolving to tell him. The next day, or maybe the day after. Maybe after she found out she was pregnant, she could just act surprised, like she didn't know how it could have happened.

But the tests kept coming back negative. Martha bought so many of those damn pregnancy tests. Wrapping the spent sticks with the double negative in toilet paper and then hiding them at the bottom of their garbage like the cigarette butts she used to hide from her parents. For months and months, it went on like that. Her periods grew harder and harder to bear. She would lock herself in the bathroom and weep.

Martha couldn't talk about it. Where would she begin? So she withdrew, began staying in bed later and later in the mornings, began losing weight. It was the first time in her life she hated being skinny.

Finally, she went to a fertility doctor. He did a battery of tests. The outlook wasn't good, but before he could decide a course of action, he wanted her partner to come in. "That's not possible," Martha said, shaking her head. "It's just not possible."

Carl noticed the change, of course. How could he not? Even as focused as Carl had been with work, he knew something was wrong. Martha's hair lost its luster, her eyes dulled and grew distant. She was getting so thin.

He asked her all the time. But she kept shrugging it off, denying there was a problem. Carl tried all sorts of strategies. He brought her flowers. He collected more trinkets. He cooked meals. But Martha barely ate. None of the gestures helped.

Then the sex stopped. And once that happened, Carl demanded they talk, that she tell him what was going on.

"It's not you," was basically all she could manage. "I swear, Carl. It's not you." She didn't know that for sure. But that's what she came to believe.

One morning, Carl went into the bedroom to wake Martha up. He opened the door. She was sitting in bed staring blankly at the wall, still wearing the loose sweats she'd slept in. Her hair was a mess. Carl sat down beside her, tried to pull her toward him, to hold her the way he used to. Her hands were cold. Her body felt limp in his arms. She wouldn't make eye contact with him, wouldn't let her kiss him. He tried to tell her it would be fine, whatever it was, but he was becoming less and less sure that was true. He kissed her closed eyelids.

She turned her head away and wiggled out of his arms. "Don't," she whispered. "Please don't."

Carl was scared. "Martha, come on! Please talk to me. Just tell me what it is!"

Martha was trapped. She wasn't sure what to do anymore. "I can't, Carl. I can't do this."

"What? What can't you do? What are you talking about?"

She didn't answer. She left the room and locked herself in the bathroom. He followed her. Through the closed door, he tried again. "What are you saying? What can't you do?"

She didn't say anything. Behind the door, she stared into the light bulbs above the mirror, looking at them until they burned her eyes, until she couldn't take it any longer. Then she looked away and leaned into the mirror, blinking hard, seeing only her negative image.

"Anything," she finally said. "Nothing."

"I don't understand." His voice was pleading but growing more and more impatient. "Are you leaving me? Martha, this isn't…"

"I went off the pill," she finally blurted out, interrupting him. "Okay?" She opened the door to look at him. Her eyes were red and tired.

"What did you say?"

"The *pill*, Carl. Birth control. I stopped taking it."

He was so confused. He started to ask, but she continued, tears forming.

"Something's wrong with me. I can't…we can't have a baby."

At first he was silent. As far as he knew, they didn't even want to have a baby. They weren't trying. It didn't make any sense.

"But I thought…"

"It doesn't fucking matter. None of it matters anymore."

"Wait, wait," he tried, searching for something to say. He looked at her. Shoulders sagging. Head down. She was so fragile. She looked so exhausted.

"I wanted to have a baby with you. Okay?" Martha yelled at him. "Is that so wrong?" She began to sob.

He hugged her. At first it was halfhearted. He wasn't sure what he felt. But as she cried and cried, pounding her fists against his chest, he softened.

"I wanted to have a baby, Carl. I wanted to be a mommy. I wanted…"

He tucked her head under his chin, kissed her on the head, told her it was okay, that she'd be fine, that they'd be fine.

And for a while it seemed like it might actually be fine. Over the next several days at least, Carl was just relieved that Martha didn't have cancer, that she wasn't having an affair, that he hadn't done something to hurt her. He came home earlier from campus. He brought movies for them to watch. He cleaned the house, dusted off her curiosities, cooked comfort foods.

Martha was still wounded, though, and she remained rigid and resistant. She had no energy. Her eyes were dull. After a few weeks like that, Carl's patience began to run out.

"Listen, Martha," he said one evening after she pushed around the dinner he'd made them. "There's something I've been meaning to say."

Martha knew where it was going. Carl adjusted his glasses.

"I'm sorry about everything," he went on. "But I'm still not sure how you could have... How long were you...I mean, what if?"

Martha refused to make eye contact.

"Why didn't you just tell me?"

She kept her eyes averted. She didn't have an answer, so she said nothing. She wanted to ask him to see the doctor. She couldn't believe he didn't offer to go. So she kept her focus on the floorboards, noticing for the first time that some of the pieces of wood were shorter than others, that one section probably had been a patch job. She knew she should explain herself, but she didn't have any words. She kept her lips scrunched together.

The more Carl thought about it, the angrier he got. It didn't help that Martha wouldn't talk.

They were upset about different things and so grew further and further apart. They hardly talked. Martha would get into bed well after he already was snoring. They slept with their backs toward each other, a big pillow in-between. She often didn't get up until close to noon. Carl left the house earlier and earlier and stayed on campus through dinner. He spent all of his Sundays with his research partner.

Martha wanted to ask him what the hell he was doing over there all day, what they even talked about. *Why does he have so much to say to him and nothing to say to me?* She didn't ask. She began wondering if he was having an affair.

Martha brought more and more home off the street. A little wooden schooner appeared on the kitchen counter. A string of beads and shells hung from a hook outside the front door. The skull of a bull. A large metal scarab. After she set up the new pieces, she crawled into bed. She hid from Carl. She hid from everyone.

At times, one of them tried to reach out. But the times never aligned. One night when Carl came home, Martha went to him in the kitchen. She let her eyes go soft. She took a posture of reconciliation, with chin down and head tilted to the side. She tried to solicit pity. Looking at him, hoping he'd notice, she was ready to apologize. But he didn't notice. He brushed past her without even seeing her, got a bowl of cereal, exhaled loudly, and walked out of the room.

Occasionally, Carl resolved in his office or on his walk home that it was time to try again. He'd ready himself to apologize, plan out what he might say. But then he'd open the door and see all Martha's junk everywhere, the house a mess, dishes not done, dinner not made. Or maybe he'd see her sitting in the living room, staring blankly out the window, still wearing the clothes she'd worn to bed the night before, and the moment would pass.

Carl began to hate the clutter in the house. "*Really?*" he asked after he stubbed his toe on some rusty railroad spikes she'd found. When his toothbrush was wedged between two Conch shells, he yelled at her. "Don't you think that's enough, Martha? Isn't it more than enough? It's getting hard to breathe in here!"

One Sunday when Carl came home he found a Styrofoam brontosaurus beside their mailbox. That was the final straw. It was the last thing he wanted to see. It was ridiculous, like some grade school art project. In a rare outburst, he actually chucked his bag up toward the house and cursed. Martha heard the bang and so came out to see.

"What the fuck is this?" he yelled.

She flinched but didn't respond. When she brought it home from a yard sale that morning, she had held a small hope that Carl might actually like it, that maybe it would make him laugh, would at least break the ice, might even get them out of the deep rut they were in. It was silly, still she had hoped that the dinosaur might remind him of bigger things, like the long sweep of time, like the transience of all things, or something. At least that's what it did for her.

"Forget it," she said in frustration.

"Forget it?" he exploded. "How the hell can I forget it? It's awful. Looks like some kid made it."

"Oh, just shut up!" she said and slammed the door on him.

Carl ran up the steps and threw open the door. "No! No, I won't shut up. I've been shutting up too long now. I want it to stop. All of it. I want it out of here! You're turning my house into some roadside attraction. It's a fucking embarrassment."

Without looking at her, he retreated into the spare bedroom, the one that would have been the nursery. He shut the door as hard as he could. She jumped at the sound.

A WEEK LATER AROUND dawn, Carl was wide-awake. Martha was still in bed. The dinosaur was still out on the curb. Carl got dressed for work, grabbed his bag and left the house. The sun had yet to rise, and the dark air was cold and damp. As he got to the dinosaur, he pulled an index card out of his pocket and wrote *FREE* on it, bent down, and left it leaning against its front left leg.

Nobody's going to take this piece of crap, he thought as he walked off toward campus. *But what the hell.*

To Carl's amazed delight, though, the stupid thing was gone when he came back late that evening.

"Jesus!" he said, picking up the mail, grinning as he opened his front door. "That was easy."

Martha didn't know what had happened or where it went. She assumed Carl had flung it into a trash bin somewhere. She didn't ask. Figured it was better to act like she didn't notice.

But she did notice. It broke her heart. She missed the dinosaur terribly, and she was furious at Carl. Felt like she had let the woman down who had given it to her, that she was a failure for not providing it a good home.

Good thing you didn't have a child, Martha scolded herself. *Can't even keep a sculpture of some dinosaur safe.*

She began hunting the neighboring blocks, hoisting herself up onto the lips of dumpsters, peering down the alleys behind restaurants and office buildings. She thought about posting a sign, even offering a reward. It was nowhere to be found.

Meanwhile, Carl felt lighter than he had in a long time, buoyant even. He eliminated a few other items Martha had gathered. He carried the broken schooner out to the curb and placed a similar sign in front of it. Someone picked that up as well. He even got rid of Eugene, the porcelain elephant. It seemed there was someone out there who would take just about anything.

They were heading in opposite directions. Over the next couple weeks, Carl removed a piece at a time from the mess that had become their lives. A box of shells went. He got rid of some *Wizard of Oz* anniversary plate and the dented diving helmet.

Martha started frantically hoarding more, bringing anything she could home. She hid the new pieces in her walk-in closet. She found a set of pins commemorating each Apollo mission in the free box at a church rummage sale. A model of the solar system. An old, rusty saxophone. She brought them in when Carl wasn't around, and she packed her treasures away. Her closet was overflowing.

After Carl left for work each morning, she'd take them all out, setting the house up the way she'd have it if she lived alone. Out came the pins and plates. Out came the lighthouses. Out came the sea glass.

Those were the happiest times Martha had. Sitting alone among all her treasures. Coffee in her cup. For a few hours every day, her life felt momentarily full. But as the light shifted across the windows on the east side of the house to the windows on the west, she knew she had to hide it all again. Back in went the driftwood. In went the figurines. The crystals and postcards. One by one, she would return each piece quietly to her closet.

It went on like that into the fall. Carl had moved onto the couch in the spare room. Inertia, or maybe fatigue, was all that was keeping them together.

THEN THE EARTHQUAKE HIT. The roof of the Philosophy Hall caved in. Carl's lab was ruined. Martha's favorite things slid off shelves. Many of them shattered. The city was a wreck. Everyone wondered if the new bridge would hold.

Despite it all, despite everything they'd been going through, Martha and Carl both immediately worried about each other. Carl tried to call but the lines were down on campus, and his cell phone wouldn't complete the call. He rushed home.

For a moment, it seemed like things might get better. Carl was so relieved that she was okay. "My lab is ruined," he told her. "Lost a lot of work. Buildings are definitely going to be closed for a while. It was really scary up there."

Martha tried. "I was so worried about you," she said. She wanted to hug him. But his body felt different to her, like he'd started working out. She had trouble looking at his face. She retreated again.

Carl retreated, too. But not fully. Something in him opened a little, something shook loose. And over the coming weeks he began thinking more and more about who they'd been before, about how much he had loved her, how much he still loved her. He began searching for a way back.

Just before Christmas, as lights went up around the city, as trees were dragged into living rooms, Carl glimpsed what it might have been like to have a child, what it might have been like to raise a child with Martha. Then he pictured Martha alone in their house, how isolated and fragile she was, how thin she'd become.

It got to be too much to bear. Carl felt it like a sudden downpour. Life was too short. This was it. She was all he had. He was all she had. He couldn't let her slip any lower, couldn't let himself slip any lower.

He walked quickly back from campus that afternoon, trying to think of something to say, how to make things better. Flowers certainly wouldn't be enough. Chocolate wouldn't help. He needed a big gesture.

Lost in thought, trying to decide what to do, he walked right past McGee, where he normally turned. So he went down Sacramento instead, a street he rarely used. On the sidewalk in the middle of the block, in front of a gray, four-floor apartment building, beside huge stacks of yellowing newspapers and *National Geographics,* old electronics and bags of garbage, Carl saw something that stopped him dead. He adjusted his glasses. He decided it had to be a hallucination. Either that or a gift from God.

"I can't believe it," he said aloud, looking around the block to see if it was some kind of practical joke. Pulse racing, he hurried down the sidewalk, trying not to get his hopes up. He figured it must be a trick of the mind. But the vision didn't vanish. "I can't believe it," he said again. "Thank you."

WHEN CARL MADE IT home, he could see Martha through the bay window silhouetted in the early evening light. Her back was to the glass, her head downcast slightly. She was still so beautiful to him. Always had been. He swallowed hard, feeling the tears coming. He removed his glasses and wiped his eyes. Carl took the steps two at a time, knocked quickly on the door and then ran back down, just out of sight.

Martha was surprised by the knock. She hadn't been expecting anyone other than Carl, and he had a key. She walked cautiously to the door, preparing to meet a Jehovah's Witness with a *Watchtower*. She peered through the peephole. But no one was there. She opened the door slowly. Still nobody. Then she looked down. And then she saw it. There it was. About the size of a large dog, a big, red bow tied around its middle. There it was, her brontosaurus.

Carl was standing a few feet behind it. Martha's eyes rose to meet his. His hand was on his heart. Tears were running down his cheeks.

"I'm sorry, Marth. I'm so sorry."

It was all she needed to hear.

"Oh, me too, Carl. Me too," she said quickly, rushing down the steps, brushing past the dinosaur. She ran straight into his arms.

BUILDING A BRIDGE

GEORGE WASN'T ONE WHO generally appreciated change. It's not that he was a complete Luddite; he just didn't take well to the new technologies. He felt like he was being left behind. Or, rather, he felt that some part of the world was being left behind, that the real world was disappearing. With everything going digital and virtual, everything becoming temporary and disposable, George clung more tightly to what he could see and feel, things that lasted. The wind in his face. The ground beneath his feet. The ocean that stretched out to the edge of the sky.

So George could have resented the new bridge being built. *What was wrong with the old bridge?*, he might have asked. *What a waste of time and money.* But, ironically, George didn't merely like that they were building a new bridge, he came to rely on it. He needed it.

Unless it was Sunday or the weather was particularly foul, George woke up, took a shower, drank a cup of instant coffee, and ate a yogurt. Then he packed a lunch and put it into his red backpack, where he kept his binoculars and a baseball cap. He grabbed a folding chair and was out the door by 8:15. He caught the fifty-one just down the block. It took him straight down to the marina. A pier extended almost a mile out into the water. From there the view was perfect.

Bums sat out on that pier all day with boom boxes at their feet and brown-bagged forty-ounce bottles of beer angled obscenely between their thighs. Some dozed beside their slack fishing lines. White sails speckled the water and raucous gulls screeched and swooped overhead. Delicate sandpipers hopped around on the shore in search of scraps and snails. The big ships went out, and others came in and then went out again. The ones coming in from China were loaded with electronics, machine parts, or plastic pellets. The ones going out were filled with fruit and nuts, wine, dairy. George preferred the cargo that was leaving to that which was coming in. Every exchange felt to him like a bad deal. But he tried not to focus on all that.

George went down there to watch that great bridge being built, its steel immensity daring to stretch toward the opposite shore. Even with all those men in hard hats working, even with all those cranes on the barges swinging back and forth, it was hard for most people to detect any change at all from one day to the next. For years the damn thing had been under construction, the rhythmic pounding on the pilings could be heard miles inland. Most locals had long given up hope it would ever be done. George heard the people moaning about the pace of the project in the coffee shops and on the radio. They went on and on about it just like they did about the traffic, the pollen, the lack of rain.

But George didn't see it that way. George actually preferred the pace. He could spot the changes. He knew that the bridge was getting ever closer every day. To George, the pace was appropriate, necessary. Anything quicker would have been reckless, would have been sacrilegious. A project of this magnitude, this daunting, should move imperceptibly slowly. Like the passage of time itself or the growth of an evergreen, like the span of a life or the length of a marriage.

The goal seemed unfathomable, almost infinite. It remained a little like a dream, an expectation, a promise. And that was what George needed, something so far off that he didn't have to think about what was coming next.

He needed the sea air, too. The smell of brine and fish and the occasional spray that splashed up against the side of the pier and tingled his cheeks. He needed the wild, carefree song of the gulls. He needed to fill each of his senses, needed to overwhelm them.

A FEW MONTHS BEFORE George started going down to watch the bridge, his wife had left him. Twenty years they'd been married. Then one morning she woke up and announced she was leaving. And, to make matters worse, she was leaving him for a woman.

George hadn't seen that coming. Not at all. Even in hindsight, he found no signs. And that made him question everything he had assumed was true. *Women*, he decided, *didn't operate in the same world as he did.* Maybe no one operated in his world.

When he opened his eyes that morning, George knew immediately something was wrong. Julie was already up and dressed, was sitting on the edge of the bed. She was never up before him.

"I think I'm done, George."

That's how she did it. No opening to work it out. That was it. And then came the double shock that Julie was moving in with their friend Erika. *For how long had that been going on? And of all people, Erika!* George didn't even think Julie liked having Erika sitting across a coffee table, let alone…well, let alone a lot of things.

But he couldn't let it alone. George kept turning it over and over in his mind. He couldn't sleep, couldn't make sense of it. It drove him mad.

What had he done wrong? George was an honest man. Never cheated. Rarely lied. George had been a traveling salesman when they had started dating, one of a dying breed of men who went door to door, mostly in the more rural counties and mostly to older customers. That's what his father had done, and occasionally George would accompany him on his route. When his dad retired, George took over most of his clients.

But Julie didn't like how much George was away, and she didn't like thinking what might happen in the private homes of strangers. So George ultimately gave it up. Sure, he knew there wasn't a future in that line of work anyway. He'd been selling less and less, feeling more and more redundant and irrelevant. Still, though he never once said it to her, he resented Julie for urging him to stop doing what he loved.

George took a course at the community college and became a Certified Bank Teller. For fifteen years, he'd been working at the credit union downtown. For the last five, he'd been the manager of the place. He was not proud of the job, but it paid the bills, and it kept him close to home.

❖

AFTER JULIE LEFT, GEORGE took two weeks' vacation from the bank. He couldn't muster up the energy to count money, to smile at people. Everything became hard for him. Small tasks: taking out the trash. Running errands. Even brushing his teeth. Drying off after a shower. Shaving. He hated seeing himself in the mirror.

His hair went from salt and pepper to just salt. The bags beneath his eyes became purple and pronounced. He had only just turned fifty-eight, but George seemed to look older and older each day.

One morning, a friend dragged him out to take a walk down by the marina. George spotted a huge piece of equipment floating on a barge under the bridge.

"The hell is that for?" he asked. Neither had a clue what it was.

"That old thing?" the friend said when they were back on the bus and George was still talking about it.

"Must be something for the bridge."

"Gonna take a lot more than some piece of crap on a barge," his friend barked, "if they ever want to finish it."

George hadn't argued at the time. But his curiosity was piqued. He went back the next day to take a closer look. Turned out the barge was hauling a massive hydraulic pile hammer. And indeed it was for the bridge. That pile hammer, he soon learned, was about to drive a piece of reinforced steel deep into the bedrock almost 300 feet below the surface of the water. It would ultimately help all the other piles hold up that big bridge. George couldn't fathom the strength required to drive that pile way down into the crust of the Earth, let alone to hold up a bridge. Lately, he'd hardly been able to hold himself up.

George kept heading back there. He went after his shifts ended or on his days off. At first it was maybe once or twice a week, and only for a couple of hours. But he started staying longer and longer. He took sick days. Soon it became the only thing George looked forward to.

Eventually, summer came, and George quit his job. It was the boldest decision he'd made in recent memory. He had enough in savings to live for a while. And he figured he could get a job at another bank when he was ready.

He began going to the water every day. He found a spot on the pier that offered the best view. He became obsessed with what was happening. He even began to anticipate what the crew would work on the following day.

George appreciated the beauty and quiet grace of the design, the simplicity of the single pentagonal tower, the subtle arc of the main cables, the gentle curve of the deck. It was crisp and clean and somehow feminine. But it was strong, sturdy, and reliable, more reliable than anything else in his world.

Just as he had his favorite features, he had his favorite workers. He watched them through his binoculars, and he began to recognize their faces. Most of the crew was young, except for the guy with long silver hair who looked at least George's age. That man was a recent addition to the crew. George had noticed his arrival because he was so much older than the others. He had some job on the underside of the span. He was up there on the scaffolding or suspended in a harness a lot of the time. George liked to imagine being in that guy's place, the wind in his hair, his hands pressing against steel and concrete.

George read everything he could find about bridges. He went to the library and took out book after book. He learned about the particular challenges of this bridge, like the structural requirements and how the bearings and shear keys had to allow the span to give and move in an earthquake. He read about the load on the main cables, an almost unimaginable burden they had to bear. He became an expert on the different booms on the various cranes. And he was there, of course, when one of those cranes tipped over and crashed into the water. George felt the accident personally and powerfully.

The drunks on the pier would slur and swear at him sometimes. Harass him a little.

"What's you looking at today, Pops?"

Mostly George ignored them. But if they pushed, he might nod his head toward the construction and mumble, "That bridge out there."

"Aw, that damn thing?"

"That very one."

"Why you watching that for?" they'd ask.

"Don't really know," George would say after a while. And if he was in a particularly foul mood, he might add, "Well, what you fishing for?"

If George really tried to explain what it was he saw in that bridge, why he was watching it, they would quickly lose interest. It wasn't something easily understood, certainly not easily articulated. The building of that bridge simultaneously calmed and excited him. It represented the best in mankind.

Real water was out there to be crossed. That's what George wanted to say. Even if the engineers used new computer models and simulations, that span, made of real steel, was the only way to cross it. And real workers were out there building it. They all existed in the real world. They used real tools, held them in their real hands. They spread out real blueprints. It took real time.

Same concepts went into building the bridges in Rome, he would have liked to tell the fishermen. *Sure, technology's changed. But the problem's the same. The physics hasn't changed.*

❖

IN EARLY FALL, AS the bridge neared completion, George found himself getting increasingly agitated. He left his hat at the marina one day. He cut himself shaving. He lost his wallet.

At first George was worried that something would go wrong, that the final pieces wouldn't connect, that the bolts wouldn't hold. He feared the plans somehow had been drafted incorrectly. He worried an earthquake would knock it down. Maybe the engineers had underestimated what a big one would do to the load bearing points.

But the days rolled on, the work continued, and it all progressed smoothly. So George's worry flipped: He feared nothing would go wrong. The final pieces would connect perfectly. The crane arms would retract. The barges would come to carry them back to where they came from. The workers would go home. The ribbon would be cut. The cars would come.

And that's just what began to happen. The pieces fit. The cables held. The lights worked. The lane lines were painted. Scaffolding came down. Trees were brought in for the median. Fewer and fewer workers showed up each day.

George began biting his nails. He hadn't done that since he was in high school. He chewed a few of them down so low the cuticles started bleeding. He was thinking of Julie all the time. The less activity there was on the bridge, the more she was in his brain.

❖

GEORGE HAD INTENDED TO go down to the marina every day until the ribbon-cutting ceremony. But, one day, he decided he'd had enough. There was no point in going again. That morning, he was still in bed when the fifty-one hissed to a stop. George pulled the blanket up over his head and heard the bus drive off without him. He hadn't said goodbye to anyone on the pier the day before. He didn't think anyone would even notice he wasn't there.

After that, George didn't know what to do with himself. He didn't want to go back to work. He went to the library. He did errands. The drugstore. He shopped slowly, trying to pass the time, to get through the day.

The supermarket had to be George's least favorite place. He struggled not to feel sorry for himself as he wheeled his cart around. He bought mostly canned goods, cereal, applesauce, single-serving yogurts, foods that were easy to prepare, easy to eat. He would pass women buying big sacks of flour, family packs of chicken, watermelons, tubs of peanut butter, and gallons of milk.

He could feel the sorrow come over him sometimes. He felt it in his jaw, in his upper chest, and he didn't need to see himself in the butcher glass to know that he looked like a lonely man.

A few days before the bridge was set to open, George was in the supermarket. It was late autumn, but the rains still hadn't come. He glanced at the headlines of the local papers as he entered the store. They were all about the bridge and the drought.

Well, I guess they did it, he thought, with a shake of his head. *About time, I suppose.*

He pulled a cart out and wheeled it into the store toward the cereal aisle. Suddenly, George felt a sharp shock in his left hand.

"Ah!" he hollered, shaking his hand and bringing it toward his mouth. "What was that?" A row later it happened again. "Jesus!"

A stout woman heard, scowled at him and steered her cart around his.

Every ten feet or so, the shooting pain came again. He would feel it first in one of his hands and then the electric shock would shoot up his arm. The first few came as a surprise. But soon he started anticipating it, almost a worse sensation. He feared he was experiencing the first signs of a stroke or heart attack.

He shyly approached a younger woman in the produce aisle. "Sorry Miss, but are you getting buzzed?"

Buzzed wasn't the word he'd been looking for, and she eyed him suspiciously. "Pardon me?"

She appeared to take the line as a strange come on, like George was some creep who came to the supermarket to flirt with female shoppers.

"Oh," George stammered, realizing. "No, no. I didn't mean…"

"Sure you didn't, you weirdo."

George quickly pushed his cart away, mortified. And soon he was shocked again. "Damn it!"

She looked back and shot him another nasty look.

The heck is wrong with this place? George wondered.

The other shoppers began to stare. They gave him a wide berth, chose different aisles. He stood still momentarily, trying to gain his composure. He looked down at his mostly empty cart, tucked a side of his button down back into his pants and then rubbed his rough face.

Eventually, George sighed and started down another aisle. When it happened again, George thought he saw a spark fly. He cursed, and when it happened another time, he cried out, "Stop! Please, stop!"

George figured he should exchange the cart. *Yes, it must be the cart*, he decided. He carefully rolled it toward the exit. He unloaded the items into a new one, as a clerk and a gaggle of other shoppers stared. The small box of All-Bran, the prepackaged sliced ham, the cans of soup, the Dannon, the can of corn, the macaroni and cheese, the green grapes, the toilet paper. They all went into his new cart.

George felt the eyes on him and was ashamed of the inventory, felt like his whole pathetic life was on display. He pushed the cart off quickly. After maybe four steps he was shocked again. He pulled his hand back hard.

"Fuck!"

George wasn't one to curse, he said it with as much self-pity as rage. But the store manager heard and approached.

"Is there a problem, sir?" The manager had an arrogant, sibilant voice. He wore a striped skinny tie with a poorly-tied knot. He had a lot of product in his thinning hair.

"Yes. Yes. There is a damn problem," George said.

"Look, sir, this is a family establishment, you see? We have women and children in here, you see? I'm going to have to ask you to leave if you can't control yourself."

George was flabbergasted. *Ask me to leave? Why the hell am I being reprimanded? And why the hell does this guy keep saying, "You see?"*

"No, *you* see," George yelled back, uncharacteristically. "I'm in total control!" His voice cracked with emotion. "I haven't done anything wrong! It…It's your carts that are the problem. They're shocking me to high hell!"

The manager raised a single eyebrow. "Okay, okay. Easy does it. Let's give it a look, shall we?"

His tone made George want to knee him in the balls. He hadn't felt that impulse in a long time. He pictured going through with it, planting his knee cap solidly into this man's pompous groin. He imagined the other shoppers clapping, maybe the supermarket would see him as a liberator and give him his groceries for free. But George knew better. He held back and instead considered just leaving the store. But he had nowhere else near his house to shop. If he left, he'd have to just come back later that day or the next.

The manager took the handle and rolled the cart away from George with a kind of bravado, pinky fingers upturned like he was holding a wine glass.

This idiot thinks he's better at pushing carts than the ordinary customer, George thought in disbelief. He did a spin around the banana display and parked the cart back in front of George. Didn't get a single shock.

"Seems perfectly fine to me, you see. Would you like me to get someone to wheel it around for you?"

George was mortified. "No, I do *not* want someone to wheel it around for me! I'm not a child! I'm not some invalid!"

"Well, then you must calm yourself, sir. Consider this a warning."

A warning? The bastard thinks I'm six!

George walked away. His neck felt itchy, like he might be breaking out in hives. He tried hard not to touch the metal, keeping his fingertips only on the yellow plastic handle strip. It was awkward and made it almost impossible to turn. He bumped into a shelf. Then into someone else's cart. Backing up, his hand slipped onto the metal again. He immediately was shocked. He winced but held his tongue.

Next, George tried pulling down his sleeves, covering his hands with the cuffs of his shirt. This was even more awkward, but it worked. That is until he extended his hand and picked up a tin of tuna. He got such a shock, he dropped the can.

George's anger was gone, replaced by resignation, then sadness. He stood there, paralyzed, not touching anything, looking around for a kind face. Even for Julie. What he would have done to see Julie right then. His hands were trembling. He bit at his nails.

Just then, George felt a delicate hand on his shoulder blade. He sprung back at the touch.

"Try taking off your socks."

"Excuse me?"

He turned to find a woman, in navy slacks and a white blouse. Her long hair was pulled back. She looked a bit like Georgia O'Keefe before all her hair went white. She pushed a shopping cart half-filled with cleaning supplies.

"Yes. Happened to me once before. Are they wool?"

"Are what wool?"

She smiled. "Your socks."

"Don't know. Could be." He bent down. "Yes. Well, yes, I guess they are. Bloody hell. Is that what it is? The socks?"

"Static electricity." She stepped around her cart. "Can be quite powerful when it wants to be." She smiled and offered her hand for balance while he reached down and removed a shoe and then the thick sock. "Particularly when it's been dry." They switched hands, as if in some strange tribal dance, and he undid the other shoe and pulled that sock off as well.

George blushed a little. It was the first contact he'd had with a woman since Julie. "Thank you," he said finally.

"My pleasure. I'm Rose."

"Now they'll probably throw me out of here for not wearing shoes."

She laughed, but she didn't let go of his hand.

"My name is George." He moved her hand up and down in a shake and tried to look her in the eye. "It's nice to meet you, Rose."

They let go of each other's hands then. George balled up his socks, tossed them in the cart, and then he put his shoes back on. They continued down the aisle together. He didn't get shocked again.

"Ah, that's good," he said. "Never enjoyed pushing a cart so much." She laughed. He thought she had a nice laugh.

George wasn't sure what to say next. They were side by side, moving slowly down an aisle, George yielding if another shopper came the other way and then catching up again. Rose bought a package of oatmeal cookies and a box of Earl Grey tea. He bought some Ritz crackers and a jar of Folgers. Shopping together is an intimate affair, and he didn't want to make her uncomfortable.

"Shopping for your husband?" he asked, and then kicked himself for prying.

"Oh, no. Henry passed," she said. "I live alone."

"So do I. Still getting used to it."

"I've been doing it for years," she said and then forced a smile. "You get used to it, I suppose." Her voice trailed off as they neared the end of the aisle. "But that doesn't mean you ever really like it."

There was silence then, and George figured she'd go the other way. When she didn't, he searched for something else to ask her.

"They're about done with the bridge," he said eventually. She didn't say anything, and he once again regretted what he had said.

Rose looked lost in thought but then perked up. "I know. Never thought they'd get all the way across."

"Amazing isn't it?" George said, hopefully.

"Quite. Sad, too, in a way, I suppose."

George looked at her in surprise and then nodded. "Yes it is, Rose. Yes it is."

They were nearly done shopping. He wasn't sure how to part. "If it's not too forward," George said, "what would you say to coming with me to watch the ribbon cutting? I know a great spot down by the marina where we can watch through my binoculars. It's on Wednesday, you know."

She looked at him for a few long seconds and then smiled. "That sounds lovely. Let's do it."

Saying goodbye then was easier, for it wasn't really goodbye. They planned where they would meet. George said he'd make them sandwiches. Rose said she'd bring a thermos of iced tea and some cookies.

❖

WHEN GEORGE GOT TO the bus stop Wednesday morning, Rose was already there waiting. She wore a flowered dress and a silk scarf in her hair. George thought she looked lovely, but he didn't say anything. Just smiled.

"I've only taken the bus one other time," Rose told him. "It didn't go so well."

"Well, you don't have to worry today. This is the one I always take, and we're going to the end of the line."

They shared a seat, their legs touching slightly. Rose noticed and didn't pull away.

"My wife lives down that block now," George told her as the bus crossed Valdez. "With another woman."

"Oh, George."

"It's okay," he tried. "Well, no. It's not really okay. But it's life, I suppose."

When they got off, he walked her out along a path that led to the pier. A strong smell of licorice filled air.

"Wild fennel," George said when she asked. "And that's all yarrow." He tore off a few bright yellow sprigs and handed them to her. She poked one through her pulled-back hair.

They found a bench near his usual spot and sat down. It was a beautiful day. He recognized a few of the bums but didn't acknowledge them. A soft breeze blew, not enough to disturb the surface of the water but enough to keep them cool. George shared his binoculars. Rose said the view was magnificent.

"I can't believe I've never been down here."

"It's a special spot."

The ceremony on the bridge had just begun.

"I bet the mayor's talking now," George said handing over the binoculars.

"Probably has already forgotten how long this has all been going on. Talking like it's been a smooth success."

"Without a hitch," George said sarcastically. "Water under the bridge."

"Seems like they're about to cut the ribbon," she told him, passing back the binoculars.

"Just like that," George said as the two halves of the ribbon fell to the roadway. "So it goes."

They watched the people clear off. And in what seemed like just a matter of seconds, the cars came rushing across. "Well, what do you know," he said.

"What do you know," Rose repeated.

"Here they come," George told her. "How'd they get there so fast?"

"Must have been lining up on the Interstate waiting, I suppose."

George pressed his eyes even harder into the rubber eyecups. The cars whizzed across. "What the hell's the big hurry?" he whispered.

Rose shrugged her shoulders. "Guess that's why you build a bridge."

George smiled to himself wondering how he didn't think about the cars that would be driving across. He never really pictured the bridge being used.

"Wouldn't do much without cars," he said eventually.

"Guess not," Rose said.

"Should be proud or something," George continued. "But I'm not."

"Hard not to pity the old bridge," Rose suggested. "Looks like it's given up, doesn't it? Like it's about to fall into the water."

"God, you're right. Was doing fine yesterday. Even just an hour ago! Was needed then. Now it's like a dinosaur."

George took up the binoculars again. "Man, look at them race across. They don't even think about it, do they? Seems a little disrespectful doesn't it? It's going to take them less than a minute to reach the other side."

"Let's time it," she proposed.

And so they did. They sat counting the seconds it took a blue car to get from one side to the other.

"More than ten years to build and only sixty-five seconds to cross," George said, shaking his head. "That doesn't seem right, does it?" They sat there side by side for a while, not saying anything.

"That's life, in a way," Rose said eventually, almost to herself. "Henry's been dead longer than we were married."

George looked at her then and, after a few moments, cautiously slipped his arm around her shoulders.

"Amazing how time passes, how it all passes."

They watched the cars zoom across. Rose raised her hand and laid it on his. George felt a jolt of electricity course up his arm and down his leg. He grinned at the sensation.

They sat like that for the rest of the morning listening to the gulls crying out in the breeze, passing the binoculars back and forth, and watching the swells roll rhythmically under the brand-new span.

FREE AT LAST

THE BRONTOSAURUS WAS JUST the beginning. A harbinger. A John the Baptist. In the months following its arrival, Russell's whole world seemed to change. All the patterns and routines were upended.

Maybe a month after Russell found the dinosaur, he almost hit the numbers. The Pick 6. Russell didn't actually buy tickets, he just picked the numbers. He always wrote down the combo he would have selected on scraps of paper. He kept weeks and weeks of the scraps folded up in his shirt pockets. He watched the six o'clock news to hear the numbers called, to see if he would have won, had he actually bought the ticket.

Russell never came remotely close. On a good day, he might get a few numbers right, but they were never in the correct slots. In fact, even if Russell had played every combo he'd ever picked each and every night, he never would have won. But there he was that night, following the balls as they fell out of that metal cage, and he nailed the first five. As he watched the heavily made-up Lottery girl call out the fourth and then fifth numbers, Russell unknowingly scratched his arm until it started to bleed. He felt his chest tighten, thought he might have a heart attack. He clenched his fists and pumped them into the air. When the sixth ball fell, his chin fell as well, but only momentarily.

"Criminy," Russell breathed.

His disappointment was short-lived. He ran the piece of paper with his numbers written on it right out to the balcony to show the dinosaur. "Will you lookee here!"

He could hardly get the words out as he explained how the game worked and how close he'd come.

"Maybe we ought to go to Reno, you and me. Haven't been there in years. Heck, you might have passed through Reno back in the day, no?"

Russell laughed hard at the thought. He removed his glasses and collapsed onto his chair beside his friend.

Each day brought something different. One morning he decided to wear a suit. "Well, take a gander at this!" Russell said as he thumbed through the clothes in his closet. "Haven't worn you in years."

It was the only suit he owned. A light-gray three-piece job with navy pinstripes. Russell had no real reason to own it anymore and even less reason to wear it that day. Still, he went with the urge. The fit was tight, the pants a bit short, but that didn't stop him from wearing it on his walk that morning, right under the bomber jacket.

"Strange," he said, eyeing his ankle bones as he left the building. "When would I have grown taller?"

Out on the street later that morning, he was more social than normal, like he wanted to show off a little. When the garbage men came around to take the cans, Russell went out to meet them. One of the workers nodded in greeting.

"A man can't grow taller at my age, can he?"

"How's that?"

"Haven't worn it in years," Russell said, holding out his arm and leg to the garbage man. "Fit back then. Always a good fit." At that, Russell whipped out a faded polaroid of him from the mid-eighties in the same suit. It was true, the suit fit great. "Don't think I could still be growing, do you?"

The man looked at the photo and then back at Russell, trying to gauge if he was kidding. "Probably not, Rusty," he said after a while. "Probably not."

They both laughed a little, and Russell covered up his wolf-like canines with his arm. "Looks good, though, man. Looks real good."

"Well, you bet it does," Russell said with a grin and turned to go back into his building. "You betcha."

On one of his morning walks, he caught himself whistling. Russell wasn't a whistler. He hadn't whistled in, well, he couldn't recall the last time. At least a decade. His lips felt strange buzzing together, and the stream of air wasn't very strong. Still, there he was, walking his usual route whistling a strain of a Pete Townshend guitar solo.

He bobbed his head along with the melody and made a couple of windmill moves with his arms.

The neighbors gossiped. Russell heard some of it. Someone even asked if he had come into money. He heard a couple ladies talking about new medication as he walked by them to get his mail.

Russell didn't mind. He felt the shift. Kind of enjoyed the attention. People were nicer to him. The kids stopped avoiding him. Eyes weren't averted. He felt famous. That made him even more social.

The neighbors didn't know about the dinosaur. That brontosaurus gave Russell new reason to get up in the morning. He took very good care of it, making steady conversation, keeping him current on events of local and national significance and filled him in on some of the major changes that had happened since his kind had gone extinct. Russell made sure he had fresh water in his bowl and saw to it that the leaves of the ferns were close enough for him to nibble at meal times.

When Russell looked back on it, though, something else had really been responsible for the change. He couldn't have known it at the time. Something shifted in Russell's universe that August. Something big. Bigger even than a brontosaurus.

❖

WHEN THE KNOCK CAME, Russell didn't answer. He couldn't possibly have imagined the banging was for him. He jumped a little when it continued, finally recognizing the knuckles making the noise were actually rapping on his door.

"Criminy, that's my door," he said. "Ah, shit. The ferns!" he added, certain that the former tenants finally had come back for their plants. It had been almost a dozen years since the two guys had moved out, yet he still assumed it was one, or both, of them out there knocking.

"Out here," he hollered, getting up from the couch and starting toward the balcony. "They're out here. Doing great. Just a sec."

But the voice that came back didn't sound a former tenant's voice. No. The voice that came back wasn't what Russell had expected at all. It was a female's voice. A little shaky. It was quiet. It was sweet. And it made no mention of potted plants.

"Russell?"

That was what that lovely, shy voice said: *Russell.* He froze at the sound. *Who could possibly know my name?*

"Russell?"

There it was again. *Now what in the heck could this lady want?*

Well, when he heard what she said next, Russell fell right back onto the couch. Hit the cushions hard. Felt like he fell right through the floor, into the very Earth below. His face went crimson. His eyes bulged. He looked up at the ceiling. Russell didn't believe in God, but he prayed to that ceiling. For strength. For anything.

"Russell, it's Lucy."

He hadn't heard that name in twenty years. It didn't make sense. He didn't understand. He tried to stop it from registering. He gripped the ripped cushions beneath him. He didn't breathe a word.

Lucy knocked again. "Russell, please. Can you just open up?"

The longer the door stayed shut, the harder Lucy found it to remain out there. What had she been thinking coming unannounced? It wasn't fair. She hadn't seen him in more than two decades. She didn't know if he'd even want to see her. She turned her back to the door, but she didn't leave. Staring at the dirty hallway carpet, she called again for Russell to at least come out into the hall.

Russell heard every word. Could hear her breathing. But he didn't respond. He couldn't respond. He was listening intensely. He was trying desperately to grasp the situation, trying to make sense of it, to put it into a box, to decide what he should do.

Must be a lot of people named Lucy, he ultimately reasoned. *This doesn't have to be* the *Lucy. Can't be the Lucy. Far more people out there named Lucy who aren't my Lucy, than the single Lucy who is.*

Russell worked madly to develop a theory that made sense of it all. But even if the brain was willing, the heart wasn't. He couldn't hold back the truth. Lucy was less than fifteen feet from him. After twenty years and who knew how many miles, only a few sheets of laminated plywood suddenly stood between them.

"I hear you in there. Come on. It's okay. Open up."

Russell eyed the fire escape and thought about making a break for it. But he couldn't move. He was completely paralyzed. He put his hands to his neck and temples. They were on fire. He hadn't felt temples that hot since the bout of dengue gever he'd gotten in Mexico, and that had almost killed him.

"Criminy," he whispered.

Lucy was still knocking. "Come on, Russell."

"Not the best time," he finally said, his voice cracking. "I'm burning up in here."

She didn't know what that meant. "Please," she said again. "I don't have anywhere else to go."

At that, he broke. He gave in. He threw his head back and pushed himself up from the couch. He walked anxiously to the door, put his palm against the doorpost.

"Christ, is it really you, Lucy?"

"Yes, Dad. It's me."

❖

WHEN HE FINALLY TWISTED the deadbolt and opened the door, Russell didn't know what to say or where to put his hands. He stuffed them into his pockets and tried to smile. He struggled to make eye contact, but he also couldn't look away.

Lucy had short, streaked blonde hair cut roughly into bangs. Some of it had been dyed blue. She had freckles and wore no makeup. A purple tank top half-hid a bruise and a tattoo of some arabesque pattern. Her eyes were light brown like his.

"Lucy," he whispered at last.

They stood there in the doorway for too long. Lucy carried a big backpack. She set it down, wondering if she should hug him or something. The hallway light was not flattering. And with his face unshaven, his hands still buried in his pockets, his eyes darting this way and that, he didn't seem very huggable.

She didn't seem too huggable, either. She was all bones. Her collarbones in particular, were so sharp. She had dark circles around her eyes. She needed a shower.

He looked at her wrists. They were so thin. He almost reached out to hold them but stopped himself.

"Your wrists," he finally said. "They're no bigger than a bird's."

It was a strange thing to say after all that time. She took it as an insult. He didn't mean it that way. She just looked so fragile.

"That's not what I meant to say. Birds don't even have wrists. Of course, that's not what I meant to say. What I meant to say is…ah, criminy, I don't even know what I meant to say."

What he meant to say was that those wrists looked just like he remembered she had when she was a tiny girl. He would hold her hand and rub his thumb across the back of one of those little wrists. She'd been only three when her mother left and took Lucy with her. Twenty-two years it had been. He had not forgotten how that little hand felt in his.

A fluorescent light bulb flickered down the hall. They were still standing awkwardly in the doorway. Russell was in no shape to become a dad, even to a grown woman. He wasn't prepared for that in the least.

"Well," she said after a long while. "Can I come in?"

❖

THE FIRST DAYS WERE terrible. Their roles were all mixed up. Russell lived like a teenager. He'd never had a visitor. And he never threw anything out. Magazines. Newspaper clippings. Bottle caps. Crosswords. Cassette tapes. Yes, he still had boxes of concert bootlegs on cassette, many of which he recorded himself. His shelves were lined with dusty books and binders, folders erupting with legal paper. Stacks of boxes filled with who-knew-what were next to piles of LPs. Dishes were all over the counters. The walls were covered with posters—Fellini films, the American flag on the moon, the opera house in Sydney.

There wasn't a bit of empty space and certainly no room for Lucy. Russell wasn't a host. He had no idea how to make her comfortable. He did give her the bedroom, however. He slept on the couch. Somehow, he thought to do this. It wasn't discussed, it just happened. But he certainly didn't change the sheets. The bathroom was filthy. The dressers were so full that the drawers didn't close. The closets, too, were crammed with old rock T-shirts, and musty sweaters full of holes. The place smelled of old newspapers, mothballs and some unidentifiable but very unpleasant odor.

Lucy saw no hint of her. No pictures of her on the walls or shelves. She didn't exactly expect otherwise; still, the reality hurt. Russell had a drawer full of old pictures, and she was in some of them. But he didn't show her those.

The worst part was, they didn't know what to say to each other. Lucy was shy and struggled to make conversation. Russell tried his best to avoid her. He never asked her anything. No questions about why she had suddenly shown up, what she was interested in, whom she'd loved, how her mother was.

Russell was jumpier than usual, leaving even earlier to go on his walks. That left Lucy alone in that dark and cluttered apartment. He would come home late. And of course, he always entered the house in the middle of some monologue.

Indeed it seemed Russell was always talking. He just wasn't talking to her. He'd blurt out random pieces of trivia, bits and facts that made her feel dumb and dull and unsure how to respond.

He talked all the time about ancient civilizations. Science, too. About the origins of the universe. He had a host of conspiracy theories he lectured her on. The Port of Chicago disaster was his latest passion.

"You think they didn't know about it up in Los Alamos?" he asked her one morning as Lucy was just waking up.

"Knew about what?" she said through a yawn.

"Port of Chicago! The cover up! The explosion!"

"Explosion?"

Russell hurried through all the relevant details covering the explosion, the casualties, the various causal theories.

"Wait, what port is in Chicago?"

"*Of* Chicago. Not *in* Chicago. Ah, criminy. Forget it."

Russell wasn't angry at her. He regretted the outburst. But he didn't apologize.

When Lucy tried to talk, words went nowhere. She felt foolish. She'd ask him what it was like outside, but the weather rarely changed, and he said as much. Then Russell would deliver his set piece about what a phony science meteorology was. If she asked about politics, he'd rant about Nixon. If she mentioned a pop song, he'd launch into a speech about how it was influenced by the San Francisco Sound. Russell was stuck in certain grooves, and it took so little to get him started.

"Do you like Mexican food?" she tried one evening. "I can make great enchiladas."

"Should call it Mayan food."

"Mayan?"

"No doubt they were dabbling in enchiladas," he explained. "We should thank the Mayans for so many things." He rubbed his eyes like he might start to cry and began listing some of those things. Lucy had no idea why he was getting emotional. Giving up, she got up from the table and left the kitchen.

She was already out of the room, but he continued. "Don't care much for them, though, no. Enchiladas that is. Not the Mayans. I love the Mayans. Not enchiladas, though. They just give me gas."

So she tried another tactic. One morning, Lucy woke early and was dressed, coat in hand, as Russell got up for his walk.

"Thought I might join you."

"What? My walk? Oh no. Not really a good idea."

"No?"

"Well, it's just a man was meant to roam alone. Like Kit Carson. That guy could be out on his own for months at a time."

"You only go out for an hour, though."

"Still."

"I just thought…"

Russell then compared himself to a brown bear, explaining that brown bears also always walk alone. "Never in sleuths," he said.

"Sleuths?"

"Group of bears. That's what it's called. Nobody calls them that anymore, though," he said wistfully.

Lucy was losing her patience. "What if the bear has a cub?" she blurted out.

Russell cleared his throat and adjusted his Russian fur hat. "Not the male's problem. That's the momma bear's concern. Never the male. The male roams alone."

"Okay, fine. Whatever."

He noticed her disappointment. "It's not you, Lucy. I just, well, I don't think you'd like it. Besides, it's all the same anyway," he tried. "I just go around the neighborhood.

You've seen it. There's nothing really to see..." Then Russell's whole face lightened, and he clapped his hands together excitedly. "Well, except for the day I found the brontosaurus. Wasn't that some find?"

When he said this, he let out a bark of a laugh and then covered his sharp teeth with his forearm. Lucy raised her eyebrows and shook her head. She didn't have his teeth. Embarrassed, he shuffled toward the door.

IT WENT ON LIKE that for over a month without any progress. The stability of living in one place, however, did help Lucy. The circles faded from under her eyes. The blue dye in her hair, too, washed out. She was eating more and didn't look quite as thin.

She found work checking IDs and signing people up for new memberships at the YMCA. It wasn't much of a job. Lots of crazy people hung around. She had to call the cops every couple of days to deal with them. But at least it got her out of that apartment. And she made a friend. They worked a few shifts a week together. She was a painter. Made these curious watercolors of frozen birds. Even gave one to Lucy. She brought it home and hung it on the wall. Russell didn't even notice.

Then the earthquake hit. It was a pretty big one. Lucy was home when it happened. The apartment shook badly. It bent and rocked, heaved and shuddered, and at first, she thought the whole building might collapse. Things fell everywhere. The power went out.

The whole city swayed momentarily. Even the newly-opened bridge seemed to stretch, like taffy. There were cars on it at the time, and everyone was afraid the cables might snap or that the bolts might break. That all those years of work would come crashing down into the water below.

But nothing snapped. The bolts held. There was a fifteen-car pileup. But, miraculously, the bonds didn't break. The bridge didn't collapse.

Russell was in the library when the shaking began. People were screaming and taking cover beneath the tables. The floor rippled and books flew everywhere, but Russell managed to keep his footing. He thought about Lucy the moment he realized what was happening. Like a captain in a squall fighting his way across the deck, Russell found his way to the front door. He was the first out. He ran the whole way home, falling at times, staying in the middle of the street, hoping like hell bricks or tree limbs or power lines wouldn't fall on him.

He took the stairs three at a time when he reached the building. The lights were out, so the staircase was utter blackness. He bumped into people rushing down and past him.

Russell felt his way to the apartment door and barged in, gasping for breath. He ran straight for her and hugged her tight.

"Oh, Lucy. Lucy, are you okay?"

It was dark. Lucy had been making coffee when the shaking started, and her fingers smelled like the grounds.

"Yeah, Dad. I'm okay. It was really scary. But I'm fine. Are you okay?

The aftershock came then, with Lucy in his arms. She leaned her head against his chest. He held her, eventually tilting his rough cheek down until it rested against the top of her head.

"Me? Yes I'm fine, too. You don't need to worry about me."

❖

THAT SCARE WAS ALL it took. Slowly, as the city patched itself back together, Russell and Lucy found ways of fitting into each other's lives, supporting each other, like two pieces of misshapen fruit leaning against one another in a bowl.

Lucy began picking Russell's jacket up off the floor before she went to sleep. She'd hang it on the doorknob for him to take on his walk. He started cleaning a mug for her and would set it on the counter when he left. Once, she bought a little potted jade plant and placed it next to the dinosaur on the porch. He left an old *National Geographic* open to a page he thought for some reason she'd like to look at. Sometimes Lucy collected jasmine and wild irises on her way home from work. She would put them in a glass of water on the table.

And one day she came home with an extra chair for the balcony. She made tea and brought it out to where Russell sat. Russell looked suspiciously at the chair.

"Tea? Ah, who drinks tea anymore? I mean, sure. Most popular drink in the world. But is that a reason I should drink it? It's bland!"

She shrugged and almost gave up but still handed it to him. "Come on, Dad. I'm sure the Mayans drank it."

He laughed loud at that, ducking to hide his teeth. "Well, you're sure right about that," he said behind his arm. "Oh, that's a good one, Lucy. And they did indeed. Probably invented the damn brew, too, though the Chinese get most of the credit. The Chinese always get the credit."

He took off his glasses and closed his eyes momentarily thinking about whether the Mayans cultivated tea, but then came back to her. "Mayans invented hot chocolate. Did you know that? Now there's a beverage."

Lucy smiled. "What's the dinosaur's name?"

"Name? Christ, I don't know. Didn't say. Not really mine to name. Do you think? I don't think at least. Probably already has a name."

"Looks like a Muriel."

It took Russell a second for that to register. Then he blurted out, "Muriel? Criminy, Luce. He's a *he!*" That made

Lucy laugh, and Russell noticed her laugh sounded a lot like his.

After that night, it became a ritual. They sat out there every evening, sipping the tea that Lucy would make. Mostly Russell lectured her about whatever was in his head. But day by day, little by little, between his soliloquies, they came to know each other.

Lucy's life had been a hard one. She dropped out of high school her junior year and lived on the streets for a while. She'd been in a string of bad relationships. The guy she'd been living with most recently was the worst of the pack. Even hit her a time or two. Got her pregnant and then kicked her out when she told him she wasn't keeping the child. That was why she came looking for Russell. She needed to recover, needed to figure out what she was doing with her life. Lucy didn't have many options.

Russell listened. Turned out, he was a really good listener. He just needed a reason to stop talking. He didn't give advice. But Lucy didn't want advice. She just needed someone who she could talk to, who wouldn't make her feel like a failure.

The evenings were calm out there on the terrace, the air cool and fragrant. There was just a hint of that vast, dark ocean rolling somewhere not so far away.

Russell eventually asked Lucy about her mother.

She took a long sip of tea and thought about ignoring the question. Eventually she said coldly, "I haven't seen her in years." It seemed she didn't want to talk about it. Russell didn't pry.

But after a few minutes, she continued. "You know, from when I was eight to maybe thirteen, she moved us like seven different times? I went to six different schools those years. That sucked." Lucy looked out across the street and laughed sarcastically.

Half-trying to change the subject, Russell pointed to a huge moon just rising over the hills.

Lucy didn't look. "I hated her," she went on. "That's why I dropped out and left home, if you could call it that. She had all sorts of boyfriends. They were all dirtbags. Probably where I got the habit."

Then Lucy spotted the huge glowing moon. "My God, look at that thing." She smiled. "That's all I know. Don't really know where she is now, and I don't really care."

Russell hadn't seen the woman since the last time he saw Lucy. He didn't know what to say. "You know you were conceived in the back of a pickup. Green Ford F-one-fifty."

"Ugh," she shuddered. "I don't need to hear this."

"Wonder where that truck is now? A real humdinger."

"A real what?"

"Unplanned, of course. Your mother definitely wasn't a planner. And I didn't plan anything back then, either. Now I do. You need to have a plan nowadays, what with how fast everything's changing. If you don't have one yet, make one. We can make one in the morning. But back then, we didn't need a plan. Ah, that was quite a time."

He stopped talking again to think, Lucy presumed, about the good old days.

"It was the tail end of the eighties. We were both high on acid. Great acid. Don't make LSD like that anymore, do they?"

Lucy wasn't sure she wanted to hear any more.

"We parked along the coast."

She was staring at the moon, trying hard not to listen.

"After a Grateful Dead concert. What a concert. What a band. Criminy, I miss Jerry. Wonder if he had any Mayan in him."

Lucy tried to change the subject.

"Hang on a sec," Russell said abruptly. He ran inside and into the bedroom. Started rifling through the drawer of pictures. He finally found one that he brought back out to the porch. He showed it to Lucy. It was of him and her mother. He wore aviator sunglasses and had huge sideburns and a mustache. She looked like a flower child.

He also found that picture of Lucy holding a big, stuffed dinosaur from some carnival. He showed her that one, too. She didn't remember it at all. But she stared at it a long while.

"When your mom took off with you, she left no trace. Christ, it wasn't as easy to find people back then, without cell phones or the damn Interweb. I went looking. Not so much for her but for you. I hope you know that."

It sounded to Lucy like he might be close to crying. She looked back down at the picture.

"It's a funny world, Dad. Not always kind." When he didn't respond, she tried again. "Hey, there's nothing you can do about it now. We can't change the past."

"But I had no idea where to look for you, Lucy." He was crying. He took off his glasses and brought his hands to his face. "I had no idea where you went."

A COUPLE WEEKS BEFORE Christmas, Lucy woke up with an idea. Russell heard her rummaging in the kitchen, starting to make coffee. He sat up from the couch, found his glasses, and rubbed his head.

"Winter cleaning today, Dad."

"*Cleaning?* Clean what? Criminy. There's nothing in here to clean."

Lucy laughed. He followed her eyes as she looked from one pile to another. He didn't say anything for a while, so she worried she had offended him. But then he covered his mouth with a hand and let out a loud laugh of his own.

Over the next several days, the two of them probably unloaded a shipping container of crap. Some seventies-era electronics went first, followed by a closet full of yellow newspapers. Books, board games, files, old clothes. The pile on the curb grew and grew until the neighbors complained it was becoming a health hazard. The apartment began to feel lighter. Everything started to feel lighter. The walls became visible in most of the rooms. The floors, too. Turned out they were hardwood and pretty nice.

"Who knew?"

"Not me, Luce. Not me."

One night, unprovoked, Russell cooked lasagna. "Haven't made one of these in years. Lasagna. Great dish. Used to make it all the time. On Sundays."

Lucy smiled. It wasn't a very good lasagna, but Lucy said she loved it and had a second helping. Russell was pleased. She noticed him watching her eat, and it made her happy.

"Kind of like an Italian enchilada, you know?" she said between bites.

Russell liked that. They both laughed. Russell didn't bother to cover up his teeth. Lucy didn't mind.

She got up to clear the table and set the lasagna pan in the sink to soak. "I'm glad I came, Dad," she said, turning toward him.

Russell didn't really know how to respond. He looked away and then walked out to the balcony. Just out of hearing range, he said, "Me, too, Lucy. I'm really glad."

The next day, they awoke to find an envelope on the floor near the front door. Someone must have slid it in. Russell figured it was a solicitation and didn't want to open it. But Lucy snatched it from him. It was an invitation. Hand-drawn.

"No, Dad. It's for you." She handed it to him.

"'You're invited,' it says. 'To A Christmas Eve Potluck.' Now what the heck is one of those? 'Free,' it says. Well, that's always good. 'Come one, come all. Bring a dish if you can. Eight p.m. Tables will be set in front of the library. With seasonal cheer, Eliza.'" He flipped the piece of paper over to see if anything was on the back. "*Eliza*? Who knows anyone named Eliza?"

He tossed the card onto the table. "Very curious," he said, thoughtfully.

"I think it's nice," Lucy said. "Want to go?"

Russell was still mulling it over. But then he said, "Of course I want to go. You should come, too. Heck, I even have a suit I can wear."

❖

THE GARBAGE MEN TOOK a round of Russell's junk from the curb, but a new pile quickly replaced the first. Russell's apartment started looking somewhat presentable. And then, just days before Christmas, Russell did something neither of them expected. He went over to the dinosaur and picked it up. Carried him right through the apartment toward the front door.

"What are you doing?" Lucy asked.

Russell jumped at her question, like he'd been caught stealing something. But he regained his composure. "Time for him to go, too."

"Your brontosaurus? Why?"

"They don't call them brontosauri any more, Luce. You know that right?"

She didn't know.

"I do. But they don't."

"Who cares about that, Dad. Where are you taking her?"

"Him."

Lucy let out an exasperated sigh.

"To the curb of course. It's time. I mean, I think it's probably time. Don't you think it's time?"

"I don't know. I mean, do you?"

He walked on with it toward the front door. "Besides, he's not anatomically correct."

"You mean the knees?"

That stopped him, and he turned back around. "You noticed?"

"Well, sure, I mean…"

"No! Not cause of the knees. Criminy, I don't mind that. Don't mind that at all, actually. Just think he's ready to move on."

"Who is?"

"What?"

"Him or you?" Russell didn't answer, so she continued. "That wasn't the aim here, Dad. You know that, right? Not to get rid of the stuff you like. Not to throw out stuff you need."

Russell smiled at his daughter, and for the first time since she'd arrived, his eyes were bright. He looked young, and Lucy got a glimpse of how he must have looked when he was a new father. He was handsome.

"I don't need him," he said finally. "Maybe someone else does, but I don't."

Lucy wasn't entirely convinced, and she showed it.

"I don't, Lucy. Not anymore." Their eyes met.

"But he seems happy here, dad."

That pleased Russell immensely, and he looked into the dinosaur's eyes. "Well, sure he's happy. You betcha he's happy. But that's not why he's moving out. It's not 'cause he's not happy. It's just that…he was made for wider pastures. *Way wider.*"

It was a good point, and Russell knew it, so he continued.

"I mean, look at that neck. Incredible, right? And those flanks. Look into those eyes. Old eyes. Older than the Mayans even. Does he look like the kind of creature who wants to spend his whole life on my balcony? I don't think so. No ma'am."

She looked at him hugging the dinosaur. It was probably how he used to hold her.

On his way out the door, Lucy could hear him talking to it, heard him whisper her name.

When Russell got to the street, he set the dinosaur out on the curb, its face to the setting sun. He brushed the back of his hand along the side of the dinosaur's cheek and then down along its powerful flank. He started backstepping slowly.

"Ah, almost forgot," he said, pulling a little index card on a string out of his coat pocket. It read *FREE*. He strung it over that long, proud neck.

Then he turned fully around and walked away from that beautiful creature, back toward his apartment, back to his daughter.

ACKNOWLEDGMENTS

A LOT OF HANDS and hearts contributed to this project. First and foremost, my wife Sarah read numberless drafts and put up with all my mutterings. She's encouraged and guided everything I've done. And my boys, Jackson and Noah, listened to these stories in early stages. They made lots of shrewd edits. Sara Houghteling was the first reader not obligated to say kind things. Without her support and advice, these words may not have seen the printed page. Luke Dorman is an incredible artist also based in Santa Fe, New Mexico. He drew all the character sketches and art for the cover. He also designed and drew my album art. His vision and creativity were a revelation. Jennifer Joel and Donn Lamm also offered invaluable insights. My mother, Sandy Friedland, is a wonderful writer and editor. Much of my love of language comes from her. She read an early manuscript and was a huge help. My father read a draft as well and made great suggestions. His steady interest and enthusiasm has been a buoy. Jono Manson recorded the songs that go with this book. His friendship and energy were vital throughout. And to my great band who got into the stories and gave their hearts to the songs: Jordan Katz, Bill Titus, Will Robertson, Mathias Kunzli. Thank you. I'm lucky to have the backing of the great team at Rare Bird, particularly Tyson Cornell who believed in this from day one. I'm also fortunate for the support and efforts of my agent, Amanda Case, and publicist, Jeff Kilgour. And a final thanks to all of you who backed my Kickstarter project. Your encouragement and dollars enabled this book and the accompanying songs to make it into the world.

ABOUT THE AUTHOR

DUBBED "A MUSICAL POET" by the *San Francisco Chronicle*, David Berkeley has recorded six albums and penned a memoir. He's been a guest on *This American Life* and has shared stages with Mumford and Sons, Dido, Adele, Ray LaMontagne, Nickel Creek, Billy Bragg, Ben Folds, Don McLean, and many more. According to *The New York Times*, "Berkeley sings in a lustrous, melancholy voice with shades of Tim Buckley and Nick Drake…as his melodies ascend to become benedictions and consolations, the music shimmers and peals." Berkeley lives in Santa Fe, New Mexico, with his wife and two young boys.